B. Wongar is highly regarded throughout the world for his stories of Aboriginal life. His works have been published in Hungarian, French, German, Russian, English, and other languages. They include *Aboriginal Myths* (with Alan Marshall, 1972), *Bilma* (1984) and a Nuclear Cycle (*Walg*, *Karan* and *Gabo Djara*). *The Track to Bralgu* has been published in the United States, the United Kingdom and Canada.

Also by B. Wongar
and available in Imprint

BABARU
MARNGIT

IMPRINT

THE TRACK TO
BRALGU

STORIES BY
B.WONGAR

Angus&Robertson
An imprint of HarperCollins*Publishers*

AN ANGUS & ROBERTSON BOOK
An imprint of HarperCollinsPublishers

First published in 1978 in the United States and Canada by
Little, Brown and Company
This edition published in 1992 by
CollinsAngus&Robertson Publishers Pty Limited (ACN 009 913 517)
A division of HarperCollinsPublishers (Australia) Pty Limited
25-31 Ryde Road, Pymble NSW 2073, Australia

HarperCollinsPublishers (New Zealand) Limited
31 View Road, Glenfield, Auckland 10, New Zealand

HarperCollinsPublishers Limited
77-85 Fulham Palace Road, London W6 8JB, United Kingdom

National Library of Australia
Cataloguing-in-Publication data:

Wongar, B.

   The track to Bralgu

   ISBN 0 207 17148 3

   [1] Aborigines, Australian – Fiction. I. Title

A823.3

Cover design and illustration by Nicole Court
utilising original artwork by Yumayna Burarwana
Printed in Australia by Griffin Press

5 4 3 2 1
95 94 93 92

"Wherever the white man trod, death pursued the Aborigines."

— Charles Darwin

Foreword

I FIND THESE STORIES very beautiful, with a beauty which I would suppose is that of the Australian desert, which I have never seen. The stories are harsh, bitter, magical, and to my untutored ears, they all ring true.

There is one theme that belongs to them all, the saddest theme I suppose of all history. In my young days it was called the Expansion of Europe. It was that strange flowering of the human intellect that took place in Europe, enabling its sailors and soldiers and later its traders and missionaries and scientists and fortune-seekers, to go to almost every country in the world, and to do pretty well what they liked, largely because of the superiority of their tools.

This superiority enabled the Spaniards to despoil

Mexico and Peru, the American colonists to conquer and corral the Red Indians, the British to rule India, the European powers to partition the continent of Africa, and the white South Africans to conquer and rule the black tribes and to maintain apartheid. One of the most terrible consequences of this superiority was the slave trade.

Australia was not immune, and these stories tell of the spoliation of the land and the aborigines. Bitter they are, but how could they be anything else? They are the stories of the destruction of one world by another. And the conquering world understood virtually nothing of the beauty of what it was destroying. It was regarded as an alien world, primitive, savage, barbarous, lacking all the genius of the West. So it was pitilessly destroyed. The cherished customs, the tribal meanings, the sacred places, all were broken to pieces by the guns and the laws and the bulldozers of the new gods.

Continuously intertwining with this dominant theme are the subthemes, the harshness, the waterlessness, the myths of creation and birth, of death and the hereafter, the dread for the black man of the white prison, the strange beauty of the dying world.

I do not know enough of the aboriginal contribution to Australian literature to know how far these stories open up a new lode of wealth. But they open up a new world to me, and what is more, the writer who does it is a master of the ancient craft.

Alan Paton

Contents

Mogwoi, the Trickster

THIS WAS IT — the end. It had not been such a bad life, after all. There had been a few sad days; otherwise it had been quite rewarding. I presume this is as far as one can go if one has sprung from an illiterate tribal chief and a mother who for her whole life hardly knew anything more than to plunge her *buidjub*, the digging stick, into the ground in search for yams.

Reverend George (born Gurg) of Riratjingu had died; the papers all over the country would write, they might even print a photo, of me; one from my earlier days, with me handing the Bible to the Aborigines. It is three days since I have gone, of course, but the Settlement is so deep in the bush that it takes days for word to reach

3

the outside world, unless the news is about a new mineral discovery or a cyclone.

Nevertheless, on Sunday, the day after tomorrow, the parishioners in many churches will be told: "The Lord has recalled his shepherd — the Reverend George of Riratjingu has left us." For the rest of the day, even for the whole week, the people will be stained by sadness. I had so many friends all over the country. Even the Queen knows me. Yes, she did, otherwise how could she have given me an O.B.E. for distinguished service to humanity? What a pity that my people, the Riratjingu mob, did not understand it — life would have been far easier for both of us.

Fame and respect are not counted here — now four days have gone by and I am still in the coffin, locked in the back room of the church. One takes care to dispose of the carcass of a crow or mouse but . . . the local whites in the Settlement are ignorant, even worse than blacks. They never try to see things the way you would like them to. Even if you beg and plead all your life, you are born a black, have to die as one, and worst of all you are buried differently from the way you wanted. It does not matter what you did all your life and that you preached the way it benefits them, once you die you are kicked back to the tribal man — no, they would not let me be buried in the ground with a decent Christian service. Every human creature on earth is allowed that. We did preach and practice it as well.

A long time ago, before the mining settlement was built, there was only one white man in the district — the Ranger. I did not see him often; nevertheless, he

4

always used to appear whenever someone in the tribe died. He ordered us to dig the hole, mumbled from his book "ashes to ashes," and finally threw the handful of soil on the corpse. We were not allowed then to send our dead off the way they wished. This angered the Riratjingu elders, but there was nothing one could do. To us the Ranger was a big boss — if you did not do what he told you to, or if you raised your voice, he would bring in the big mob of whites and they would finish off the whole tribe.

Nevertheless, on the night following each burial, the men from the tribe would go back, dig out the body from the grave, place it in a hollow log, and take it to our traditional burial ground. From then on, traditional ceremonies would be held to make sure that the spirit of the dead man would not go to the white man's world but to Bralgu. I wonder whether the Ranger ever found out that he had been tricked; certainly no one ever talked about it and how could he when every born creature in the tribe was in the queue to die.

Things have changed since then. Down at the Settlement the mining boss of CHEAT* had suddenly grown suspicious and angry. Now they are busy on the telephone and writing letters to find out from Headquarters the consortium's policy about the burial. They would have had dozens of meetings and discussions that could drag on for months, even years. It is useless to ring on

---

* Consortium of Homage Corporation, Exploration International, Alumina Conglomerate and Transcontinental Mining (fictional).

their conscience. Not one of them wants to say: Let our brother be buried, in the name of Christian dignity; he only needs three feet by six feet — after all he gave us all those mining fields of bauxite, the whole district. No, not one of them has the guts to speak; such a responsibility would be a heavy burden on your shoulder.

A few days ago I called on my friend John, the CHEAT chairman. He is down south now, at the regional headquarters and . . . this time I had no need to ask for my air ticket to be paid; the spirits move about freely.

"Do you really have to bother me?" asked John. We had not seen each other for years; yet he was somehow upset. Maybe not because of me, but the business — up in the bush, the country which once was Riratjingu hunting ground, there are still hills of bauxite left and they will remain around for years. Yet the consortium is like a tribe or a big family; some problem always pops up, not only to make you miserable, but to bring hard times for your friends as well.

"We have had a fair understanding of each other for years," I remarked; actually, not years, but decades. Since the first day he arrived at Riratjingu country as the chief geologist, and later the mining site manager, we shook hands many times, smoked and drank — we ate thousands of barramundi together — no quarrel, not even a sharp word had ever come between us before.

"You could not have chosen a worse time to go," John said.

"It was the Lord's, not my, wish."

"Come on, don't sell that one to me. Some of your

Riratjingu mob had pointed bones at you or finished you off with a spear. They still do that, now and then."

Never before had he talked to me like that. Whatever we did chat about, it was always with respect and dignity.

"Whatever happened to me will have no bearing on your mining operation. I only need three feet by six feet — it'll do for the hole."

"I am afraid . . . we could not allow burial on the leased land. It could support Riratjingu argument for land rights. The natives already roar to have some of it back."

"I am Christian."

"Are you indeed! Then why don't you try the church, they would surely help you."

Yes, I should have thought of that earlier. I had been destined for the clergy. You see, I did not do so badly in church, better than any other blackfellow; even many whites would envy me. Think of all those new souls I brought to Christianity, scores of them. The natives are poor and innocent; they have nothing to offer the Lord except their poverty. Nevertheless, all of them, their children and great-grandchildren, would be decent parishioners, and let us hope someone among their descendants will spring up into a tycoon and be able to give more.

I had to knock on the conscience of my friend the Dean of Capricornia; we had known each other for years. After all it was through his kindness that I had become ordained. "It was worthwhile," he often used to say afterward, feeling more content than proud. Why not —

the job had paid handsomely. We built a church, this one that I am in now, the best and tallest in the northern part of Australia. It looks more like a temple than a church, built of huge boulders, tons of weight in each. It was quite a job to bring them here. The rocks were scattered for miles along the seaside descending from the bauxite plateau. A Riratjingu myth relates that one of our ancestors, legendary Wudal, after chasing the bad spirits from land to sea threw those boulders after them. It happened during the Dreamtime, but don't take the story for granted — there is nothing written about it. It gave us a lot of trouble and sweat to move the boulders and if it had not been for the help of trucks, cranes and the blasting expertise from CHEAT we would never have brought them over here.

It is peace and calm here between the boulders now. Yes, it cost us a bit, I should be fair. Those walls around had eaten half of the whole Riratjingu mining royalty. The church looks so grand and spectacular, "a monument of Christian privilege," as a book describes the building — a pity I have to part with it. Yes, the other half of our royalty was safely placed in the Lord's hands — my friend the Dean had many words of praise for it — and sponsored the Eucharistic Congress, hosted by him. What an event; Christian souls of all colors and shapes poured in from all over the world. Yet that was not all; there have been many other proud days for us. We even engaged the bells from Canterbury to ring for days for the souls of the Riratjingu ancestors. We hoped to revoke them from Dreaming, from Bralgu, make them desert Wudal and Djanggawul and defect to our side. I am not sure what the result will be yet; it remains to be seen.

"What good has it brought you, George. I did pray for the peace of your soul at evening, will do it in the morning again," said the Dean apologetically.

"There is no room for a grave — the whole land is in CHEAT's hands."

"They will have to sort it out, don't worry."

"The elders are already staging the ceremony in the bush."

"They had better not dare, the swindlers, they forget they are Christians."

"The sound of the *didjeridu* and *ubar* are heard all night in the camp — the Riratjingu mob will be around soon to take me."

"What will they do to you?" the Dean's voice sounded casual.

"Place the bones in a hollow log as they always did to the dead."

"Are there any trees around? Didn't the miners clear them all?"

"They will squeeze me in a sewer pipe."

"My Lord, what a human disgrace!"

I whispered: "What about the church, there is plenty of room in the courtyard."

"One has to be a saint to be buried there. Sorry, we could not bend the rules."

What a pity there are no black saints and it looks as though the world will be without them. I should not have called on him after all; if you plead for help it should only be to those who could do something about it, like . . . yes, the Queen. Why not, I only would have to mention my difficulty and the whole world and all her humble servants would know she helped me rest with Christian grace.

I had never been in the Palace before; there was no need for it, or I would have called on her more often. It was some time since we met when she made the tour of the Native Reserve and . . . we even shook hands. She could not have forgotten me, for I presented her with a number of bark paintings, huge ones, about our mythological ancestors and old way of life. Some of Riratjingu elders did not like me giving away the tribe's belief and ever since have called me Mogwoi, the trickster spirit. Nevertheless, the Queen appreciated the gift and smiled politely. I thought she was going to do the same when she saw me again, but instead . . . she looked stiff and gloomy.

"Repeat your tag number, loudly and clearly," she said. My father used to wear it around his neck decades ago. Yet neither he nor anyone else knew how to read the numbers at that time. The Queen sounded rather strange. Not only her voice and behavior but even her shape had changed greatly. Of her body, only the head still bore some resemblance to her, but it was sitting on a large pedestal in the shape of a filing cabinet, totally immobile. Actually, a moment later I realized I was facing a bust of her placed on a computer. As I approached it she yelled loudly:

"Don't interfere with programming. State your problem."

"I don't want to go to Bralgu."

"So what, all your ancestors are there."

"It is out of your Domain, Your Majesty."

"What about a local water hole, shouldn't you go there?"

"It has been polluted with sewerage and chemicals ever since you opened that mining plant."

"Bias is inadmissible!"

"I only want . . ."

"More royalty, we presume."

"No, just three feet by six feet."

"Do not challenge the property law; make no obstruction to progress."

"Please, three by six only."

"The matter will be referred to the Royal Council, it meets in the fifth year of each decade."

Perhaps I should not have bothered any of them; the whites have their own problems to care about. After all, what is the use in trying to nag, you played your part while you lived and when you have gone the best you can hope for from those left behind is to forget that you ever knew them. It would be good if my Riratjingu men could understand this, but I don't think they will grasp the whole meaning of it; not yet. They are coming to me as though we have never been parted and are busy with details of the ceremony; not one — scores of them. They will farewell my soul as though I had never heard of the Cross or God. Maybe it ought to be that way; the sound of the *didjeridu* and *ubar* are rising louder. Before, it was nothing more than a whisper coming with

the wind from the open sea, far away, from Bralgu.
It is right here now, roaring like the storm, and will keep
on like that for days and nights.

It will not be very long now before they place me in
. . . If there is no hollow log around, the pipe, or discarded empty drums, would do. They could even roll me
in corrugated iron sheets. It does not matter anymore.

I doubt whether they will be sending me to Bralgu.
The Riratjingu elders say often when a man dies his
spirit splits in three parts: one goes to Bralgu to join the
ancestors; another sits on the bottom of the totemic
water hole and waits to be reborn; while the third, the
Mogwoi, they call it, wanders around tribal country. No,
they would not have me there at Bralgu. It is better that
way. After all that has happened to Riratjingu land and
the people, it would not be easy to face the ancestors.
The tribal water holes are leveled, but even if there are
any to be found around here I would not like to wait
there and be reborn; after all, what is there left to
spring into life for when even the hills and the rocks
have been taken away from the country. I am going to
be Mogwoi, the trickster spirit, moving around this
world, and from time to time I will call on all those I
met in life to make their time uncomfortable too.

Jambawal, the Thunder Man

THE WHITES are coming back — pouring in from the sky by plane, by helicopter, even by parachute. Soon the whole mob will be back and even more eager than they were before. The machines will begin to roll, rattle and roar and the town will begin to rise again; it will grow again like a forest, but such an ugly forest of concrete and steel, growing out of heaps of junk and rubbish. No, there's no way to outwit the whites; but the night before last Jambawal — Cyclone, the whites call him — had a pretty good try. One sweep this way and another there, and now in the whole town there's hardly a tree or a pole left standing. I can't see a single building that isn't smashed or torn by Jambawal's visit.

I'm glad he made it at last. Since they brought me

here to the island I've watched the sky and called to him. I knew he'd come someday. I knew if I called, and waited long enough, Jambawal would rise from Bralgu to sweep across the sea in such a rage that when he hit the town the white man and his houses would flutter like leaves in the air. Sometimes I climbed to the island peak, high, like an anthill there, and looking toward Bralgu I danced and sang to Jambawal — not so loud as to annoy him, but gently; just enough to remind him that he must come.

Perhaps I should have called to Jambawal more often, to make him come sooner — there's nothing left now to save from the whites. They have already cleaned the bush and bulldozed the black man's land. They have built their houses and made their graveyard — the country I knew well is ugly and strange. No black man now can point to a place and say: "Here, at the bottom of this water hole (please don't disturb), lies the spirit of our ancestor. That emu, see it, was once a black woman who burned her hands and became an earthbound bird. The banyan tree — now, that was planted by Djanggawul to shelter our people from the hot sun." Even the trampled space where we danced to call for rain when drought was long — that has been taken by the white man.

It's not for myself that I am sorry Jambawal came late, but for young fellows like Tommy and Wonbri. If Jambawal had heard me sooner there might have been something of the black man's land left for the young ones — but here in jail they don't give you much time to call on your ancestors and ask for help. In the old days the whites would chain you to a tree and leave you alone — you could stay there for days, for weeks maybe, with no food and still be happy. The ancestors from the Dreaming will care for you if you're alone long enough to call on them — and when the ancestors hear, and come to you, you're never alone again. The whites have changed their ways, though, and it's hard to call the Dreaming. Now they put a great sledgehammer in your hands, and bully you to swing it against the rocks from dawn till dark. When night comes and you're pushed into the lockup, you lie down without the strength to sigh or swear.

I should climb up to the top of the peak, now — the view from the highest rocks goes far beyond the town and I'd like to see what Jambawal has done to my country. But no . . . I'd better stay. Malug might wake from his strange sleep. He may need me; he might want to say something — to make a last wish or give me some advice before he's away to Bralgu forever. Poor bloke, he's really been unlucky — or maybe not; maybe it's a good way to die, to pass on to Bralgu. I don't think Jambawal meant to hurt Malug, though. He was after the white man and Malug got in the way; he wouldn't harm a blackfellow. Even crows and dingoes won't hurt their own kind.

I wish Malug could talk. There's so much to say and no one about to answer. Jambawal struck late at night — the best time to surprise the white man, to knock down his house, to scatter him frightened and half asleep with a Bible in one hand and a gun in the other. Jambawal must have been really angry. I have never before heard his voice so loud or felt the earth tremble and quiver like a beaten snake. He seemed to be trying to blow the sea from its bed, to roll it over the town and the white men. The roof of the jail flew away, and the walls slid down around us like a rotten fence. It was a pity the guards had gone — I would have liked to see them frightened and angry, but powerless to punish the wind. They were lucky that Jambawal came in the night, for they're never here after dark. As soon as they've locked the doors behind the five of us, away they go — rushing to the boat which will carry them across the bay to their own mob.

Did Malug say something then? It sounded as though he called — but no, I must have dreamed it. He hasn't spoken; didn't even yell for help when we called and searched for him. When the wind was high we thought he had blown away to the sea, and when dawn came we searched the rocks and the beach. But much later Tommy saw a hand, with clutching fingers, reaching from the wreck of the jail. Perhaps Jambawal meant to carry Malug clear away to Bralgu and knocked the jail in his hurry, for a whole wall of concrete and stone lay on top of him, and the rest of the building scattered all about.

It looks as if Mopoke had better luck. A big, tall blackfellow he was, with tribal marks on his chest and only a few words of the white man's talk. The police brought him in a few days ago, maybe from somewhere deep in the bush — I couldn't understand his tribal lingo but we called him Mopoke. He sat up at night, not sleeping, and maybe he called Jambawal to take him back to the bush or to the Dreaming. Looks like he made it, too. We found his shorts, this morning, on the beach, washed up by the sea. He must have sent them back from Bralgu — you don't need the white man's rags there.

Malug's moving his lips. I cleared the rocks from around his head and he seems to be able to move a little. Perhaps he's trying to speak . . . no, it's water he wants, and there's not a drop. I can pretend to be looking about for some, I suppose, but the water tank blew off its stand with the first wind and all the taps are dry. If Tommy and Wonbri were here they could look for the rock pool round the cliff; there's usually water there after rain, for a while anyway. But the boys . . . the morning after Jambawal passed they set off to swim to the town. They wouldn't listen to me. They should know better than to poke their noses into the white man's stinking mess. But they went.

After the night of the storm even the whites must have learned that Jambawal is stronger than any of us, that to harm him or his people is to risk his anger. The white man may have guns, and dynamite to blast the rocks, but Jambawal is the mightiest of all.

It's a hard climb up here, with the sun sitting on my head. Later in the day or early in the morning would be easier, but by then my thirst will pin me down. Malug might hold on a little longer. I left my shirt, soaked in seawater, around his head but it might be hours before I get back with my billy full of fresh water. Poor bugger — he's held on, in spite of what he must be suffering, for so long; I hope he lasts till I get back.

What a mess! The town looks like a huge rubbish dump; the higher I climb the more I can see. The airport is like a beehive; busier than it was during the war. The rescue work must have begun very early yesterday for the runways are clear and planes are flying in and out, flashing like spears. The whites are pretty quick to fight for their own kind. The help is even more than the airport can take, for some planes, sweeping around the sky, can't land and drop great boxes to parachute down from their silver bellies. There's nothing much left to block my view. Even the power poles have gone, so I've got such a good view I can see those boxes bounce as they hit the ground. And look at that! The monument in Freedom Square still stands, and I can see it even better now the trees around have been leveled. Captain Cook is still riding the stone waves to the shore, as safe as he was in the war when bombs flattened everything around him. That's when I should have gone to Bralgu, with my father and the rest of our people. I've stayed too long.

I can see Flat Island from here, half sunk in the mist at the head of the bay. They don't have a leper colony there anymore, but it was there before the war. Everyone on that island was black except the boss and the nurses, but though I've tried for years to remember those white people I can't call to mind one face, one word, even a glance. Maybe there wasn't a memory worth keeping. I do remember the Jap planes, though, and the bombs falling — that's when the whites took off in their boat and left us there. We never saw any of them again.

My father must have been very tall. I can't remember

how he looked, but if I close my eyes I can see myself riding on my father's head as he walked through the water from Flat Island to the mainland. It was low tide I suppose, but very few made it. Drowning was better than the slow and helpless death the island offered, though, for the whites came no more with food and water. Starve or drown, you end the same.

What a ruin the town is after Jambawal's rage. I suppose they'll keep the blacks away as they did before — after the air raid we walked a hundred miles around the bay only to be turned away without even a billy of tea for our trouble. My father didn't see it, though. We left him buried in the mud of the mangroves, and I held another's hand as we walked away.

It's very steep just here; I'd better watch my step. One slip and I'll end in the quarry so far below. You'd think the whites must eat rocks, they're so keen to dig them out and carry them away. Cook and his dinghy are high on such huge boulders that I wonder how they could have been moved into the town; to roll such rocks would take the sweat of hundreds of prisoners.

I wish I could hurry; I must have water soon. My mouth is already dry — perhaps I won't reach the pool. There are no leaves or grasses to squeeze for a drop or two of moisture . . . if I could find a frog buried in the sand there'd be water in his belly; a cut in the bark of a bottle tree gives a man a drink — but here are only rocks for company and no chance to wet my tongue.

The ridge has been cut down close to the sea here, as if a monster had risen out of the water to take a great bite from the land. The white man is so rock-hungry he will soon have moved the whole island away — and such a lot of the work has been done by me, swinging a hammer. For years the white man has been bringing me back here to the island, and often has kept me beyond the time of my sentence. It doesn't matter anymore, though; I've nowhere much to go when they set me free. The first time they locked me up . . . yes, I drank the water cascading over the boulders under Cook's dinghy. The statue made a fine shade to rest in, but I hardly had time to stretch out before a policeman grabbed me. I tried to explain that at the same spot had been the sacred water hole of my tribe, the Larrakeah people — all blackfellows, and even some of the first white men knew that. But the policeman thought I was drunk and dragged me away.

The sun is so hot and my mouth is quite dry — I'd better rest awhile. See how hard the whites are working to bring their ruined town to life. They've raised flags above the piles of rubbish but the colored rags hang down, and only move a little now and then in the breeze.

A mob of people comes spilling toward the beach, and not far ahead of the crowd races a blackfellow, running for his life. He drops the tins of food he carried, but the whites are not satisfied; they are after the man, not the food he stole. He's heading this way. Maybe . . . yes, it's Wonbri. It looks as if he'll make it — he's jumped off the rocks into the sea, and the mob of whites is left behind, shouting. Wonbri's safe . . . but there's a gunshot. There must be a policeman there on the beach; I can't see but I can hear the gun a second time and the cheering from the crowd. Wonbri has disappeared, but a loaf of bread still floats on the water, breaking apart as it soaks up the sea.

A convoy of ships is sailing up the harbor from the entrance toward the wharf. The whites are quick to the rescue with food and machines, and the wound on the city will soon begin to heal. Even Jambawal can't chase these men back to their own country.

There, on the other side of the bay, the setting sun is shining on Mission Beach. I always hoped — if they let me go away from here — to live there in the native settlement hidden in the thick bush, and sheltered by banyan trees. The whites call it Halfway, and certainly it stands somewhere between the tribe and the town. It would be . . . but no; it's gone too. Jambawal has wiped away even that. The huts are gone, and the banyan trees; the beach, littered with corrugated iron, paper and rags, looks strange and ugly. The mess has reached this side of the bay, too, and the body of a child lies half buried in the sand. It will be a long time before the white man's boats come this way.

That pool of water . . . it used to be here, just below those boulders, and held a little water after rain when all else had dried on these rocky slopes. The white man and his dynamite have been here since I last climbed the peak, though, and where the pool should be is a heap of shattered rock. I might have known that it couldn't survive the white man's ruin — just as the sacred caves and tribal places have been spoiled wherever his hand has lain.

Yet . . . yes, there it is; water seeping from a crack

deep in shadow, sliding across the smooth surface of the rock and only showing itself as it drips, now and then, from the end of a crooked twig.

Jambawal has left me behind again, in a strange country which ceased to be mine long ago.

Willy-Willy Man

Yᴇs, ᴛʜᴇʀᴇ ɪᴛ ɪs — far away beyond the mountains a huge post of dust has risen high in the air; it looks like a great spear thrown from earth and stuck in the belly of a cloud. The willy-willy is coming to take my soul away — it will soon be here.

I should call Nulumb, the boss, and tell him; he might like to see me off. He won't be angry; why should he? There're enough young fellas around to do my job, and do it faster than an old Abo. When we . . . No, Nulumb has left . . . the others have gone too. Gurund Downs is a deserted anthill — everyone's cleared out. The homestead's like an empty cave in the mountains, silent; dumb.

They could have told me they were leaving; I wouldn't

23

ask to be taken, but I could have walked up to the gate at the rise to wave them on their way. I've done that plenty of times before; once a year maybe, whenever Nulumb — Alan, the whites called him — and his missus left on a holiday. I'd open the gate for their car to go through, and as they went slowly past Nulumb would look at me and say: "Willy, now you're the boss of all Gurund Downs." I'd wave, then, as the cloud of dust behind the car rose and then settled in a mist. I couldn't see the car for long, but I could hear the engine, still, in the distance, and while I could hear that, I waved.

They must have been gone awhile, this time; the breeze has sifted the dust so the edges of the tire marks are not sharp anymore. They probably needed a few trucks to move all that stock. I was under a tree by the creek and heard the roaring engines — it sounded like faraway thunder, and I was happy to think the drought was breaking after so many dry years.

Now it doesn't worry me whether it rains or not. The willy-willy should . . . but the dusty post has gone and behind it only mist is left, drifting into the sky. Without the willy-willy behind it, the mountain is ugly; it looks like a huge carcass, dumped from above. I should forget about that wind for a while — if I think about it too much it might seem as if I'm nagging at the spirit to come for me. It'll be best to look as if I've forgotten about it, and the willy-willy will sneak in and snatch my soul back to the Dreamtime. If you dwell on it, though, the willy-willy might get angry and never come.

I'd better be busy with something; it's nearly noon, so

24

I should refill the water bags. "Level 'em up," Nulumb always said. "It's water that keeps us going."

Nulumb will come back again, as he always did. The others, the stockmen and the drivers, they might have gone forever, but not Nulumb. Gurund Downs has been home to him for his whole life; a man has only one place he can call by that name, whether he's white or black.

There's a horse coming down the rise behind the homestead — fast but crooked it comes, and slams against the rusty iron sheets of the shed. Poor thing has lived too long and lost its sight. I've ridden that horse many a time out mustering, but then it moved as smoothly as the wind, and fast enough to catch an emu. There's an end to every track, though, and fast or slow you come to that end just the same.

I wonder where the white men go when they get old. I've heard them say they'll travel to Heaven, and rest there. That's their Dreaming, but Nulumb doesn't believe in it. "Don't let them sell you that one," he told me. "Paradise should be down here, not in the sky." I should have asked him more about white man's Dreamtime, but I never got around to it. It might turn out that the Dreamtime is somewhere near this Paradise; then Nulumb and I could see each other sometimes. I would keep a water bag full for him, and if it's drought there, too, I could crush the water from tree leaves for Nulumb to drink. There will be no matches there; of course not. I'll make fire with fire sticks and . . . ah, forget about that — Nulumb doesn't like fire. He hates to see smoke, even two water holes away. Been like that all his life.

He was such a little boy when we found him, lying on the sand in the dry creek bed. It must have been long, long ago because he was the first white man we had ever seen. His parents must have been the first whites to travel up the valley, heading where? We found them dead from thirst, and the boy looked about the same until we gave him water. We called him Nulumb — "One who springs to life again."

There; he's coming — at the edge of the mountain country, near the gorge, the thick post of dust is shooting up again. I knew that willy-willy'd be back soon. It's not as big as it was before, but it's moving fast, twisting and winding as it goes, and will be even stronger shortly. Now it's swung around by the creek, and part of it's hidden by the hill; it'll come this way soon and . . . yes, here it is, great gusts of it sweeping up the dust. I'd better . . . no, there's no need to get ready yet — the dust cloud has passed again and is heading down the gully. He's calling for someone else, not for me. So close it came this time that the roar of it is still rumbling in the air.

The horse tries to rear up on its hind legs. It must have mistaken the roar of the wind for the sound of a man approaching with water. It's not so far gone that it can't raise a gallop, this wretched beast, though its head is crawling with flies. Before they left they meant to finish it off, but the stockman with the gun must have been in a hurry. Bad shot that, just to wound the poor bugger and not kill it.

When Nulumb comes back I'll have to tell him, and he'll do the job properly. He was so fond of that horse

26

he'd never let it go without oats, and if a stockman brought it in scratched or saddlesore, that bloke'd be sacked on the spot. Nulumb will come — where else would he go? When we found him he was too young to know where his old man came from. He stayed, and grew with us here. This place, Gurund, right here is his home. He's been away many times before and stayed away too long. He maybe saw plenty of places, and traveled a lot of miles, but the road always turned this way and brought him here again.

I can't feel much wind here on the ground, but it must be strong higher up — the windmill at the top of the pump tower is really going. It rattles and squeals, and you'd expect the water to gush up from the bore — but nothing comes; not a drop. That's never happened before, and it's many years since that bore was sunk. Two teams of horses they used, and the drill bit down and down. There was a whole mob of blackfellas here then, and I remember how we screamed and danced as the water gushed. "That one'll never run dry," Nulumb had said, and it didn't till now . . . but water's the same as a tree, a man or the wind — here awhile and then passes on, and the bore is dry at last.

I hope Nulumb had enough water for the trip. I taught him to squeeze water from leaves in the bush, but he was never good at it. A white man, even if he's grown up with us, can't learn to live the black man's way. So many things we tried to teach Nulumb, but it was like teaching an emu to fly.

The horse is on the move again, galloping down the slope and past the bore, where it props, rears, and

27

whinnies to the horizon. Perhaps there's a storm out there that the horse can sense, and calls to, though it's way beyond the sight of a man.

In the old days we used to call the rain when a drought was long. We gathered at a cave in the hills, and danced and sang for the rain to come — and always it came sooner or later. It never failed us. The rain comes to life from the Dreaming, the same as everything else, but sometimes it feels too lazy to travel, and then the dancing and singing helps to wake it up.

There are no blackfellas around now to make the rain-dance — I'm the last one left. The others, the whole mob of them, have gone, one by one with the willy-willy back to the Dreamtime — all of them.

Strong gusts of wind are catching the branches of the nearby trees, and dead leaves and dust are whirling toward the sky. Now there are uprooted bushes being caught and sent fluttering in the air. The willy-willy is here and the ground itself shakes with the power of the first attack. I'll close my eyes now — he's come for me at last and I am content. I feared I had been forgotten forever.

Poor Fellow Dingo

Eᴠᴇɴ ɪꜰ ɪ ᴛʀɪᴇᴅ to explain what happened to my husband the whites would not believe a word of it. No; that mob knows only its own god and holds that nothing else on this whole earth could be so right. Tribal people, the elders, they could have understood it, but now even the last of those has gone. Pingal, the Moon, is the only one still around.

Poor Kua. My poor husband. It would help if he only could say something — tell me what to do or where to go — but since morning he has spoken no word to me or to the children, and will not speak ever again I think. I wonder how he feels now he's a dingo. Last night he was as usual. There was hardly any wood around to keep the campfire going; the settlers cleared the bush long ago and the country hereabouts looks like a skinned beast. We went to sleep early, shoveling a pit in the sand and huddling together in it against the cold, Kua and me on the ends, and the children between. We had no roof to shelter us from the open sky and the night breeze would freeze the bones inside you. I could hear Kua's teeth rattling with the cold, like the pebbles in a dilly bag, but after about midnight I heard no more.

This morning, in Kua's place lay a dingo coiled in a knot and pressing against the children. The three children asked no questions though the eldest of them, a boy, is hardly ten. They all seemed, silently, to understand. Perhaps when they were born they already knew that one might be changed into a tree or animal; or maybe as they grew older they came to know that whatever shape your people are forced to take, you must still stick by them. There was not much change in Kua after all for although his body had shrunk from man's to dingo's his mind was on the family just the same. He still was ranging about sniffing the ground for signs of animals and now and then lifting his head against the wind to read what news it brought from the distance. Yet, even while so busy, Kua always kept his ears pricked to catch every sound and movement from the homestead, hardly a voice away.

The whites have an eye on everything, so the stockmen were already tossing away their beer cans and readying themselves for the dingo hunt. A hunt always begins and ends with booze though I've always wondered at such cheer when death was all about — my brothers Currong, Aranbi, Rureru, Narek, Awulla, Gunguyama and Erkoon, none of them found cheer, found even any mercy when they met those cheerful hunters.

So we walked, hurrying along the wire fence, where two camps away lay open country and a hope of freedom, for whether you are human or animal, the whites will not chase you indefinitely. If you are clever enough, whichever way they follow you, on foot or horseback or Land Rover, they finally tire of the game and withdraw unless there is a very high price on your head.

Here they are! The hunt, like a willy-willy, rose from the far distance and swept toward us like a storm, tearing the scrub and raising billows of dust. The children scooped out the sandy soil with their hands, laid the dingo in the shallow hole, and buried him, tossing a dry clump of burrs on top to disguise the spot. The job was finished just as the hunters rushed upon us.

"Which way did he go, the yellow devil," yelled the head stockman.

"To Bralgu maybe," I said.

"We are after a dingo, not one of your mob this time."

We all go the same way, but the white man would never understand that. It is so strange, and I wonder often, why the hell they bother to ask — sometimes even force words from you when they do not believe anything of what you say or do.

It must have been terribly hot down there in the sand. Kua thrust out his nose, panting, fighting for a breath of fresh air. The children, in terror of discovery, danced on the sand around the heap of weeds singing in tribal lingo but they need not have worried — with his gaze fixed in the distance the head stockman searched the spreading bushland and as he rode off only his voice was left behind:

"We'll get the bugger."

And they will, sooner or later, if we do not get out of the country.

I have never been out of the bush before and have not heard much about the place the whites call "town." It is a huge anthill, with so little room to move around that the people bump one against the other. I cannot see why such a big mob must be together; perhaps they have grown afraid to live alone.

Kua hated the place and often made complaining noises, and if there had been a choice I would have left the town to please him. We camped in a huge sewer pipe dumped at the outskirts of town, for we needed shelter; not from rain, for that fell so little that we almost forgot how it looked. No, we needed shelter from the dust. A vast plain, almost all the country in sight, was an open mine — where the whites dug rocks day and night and seemed never to be sick of them, and a cloud of dust, as thick as the night, hung over the town. So we all squeezed into the pipe for shelter. The children said hardly a word; and certainly there was nothing very cheerful to talk about. Kua grumbled and growled for hours on end and he would prop against me, scratching my skin with his front claws as if he was trying to tell me something, though whether it was a warning of coming danger or just his unhappiness with the new place and our situation I never knew. During the night he would squeal and shiver in his dreams, often so loudly that he woke the children. Luckily he was quiet, for to bark or howl could have brought the packs of town dogs — terriers, hounds and Alsatians — in search of him. Not that he was scared of them but he knew that he was hopelessly outnumbered by the white man's beasts, each of which was twice his size. When the dog pack came by during its wanderings Kua always backed into the entrance of the pipe, bristling his fur till he seemed much greater in size, but keeping quite silent. With the mob gone by, however, he would rush out, circling angrily to lift his leg and leave a mark on every log and rock, on stumps and even on the thistles.

There was no bush food to be found around. From the mangled dusty earth even the insects had vanished. Now and then Kua would drag home a large bone from the rubbish dump, but there was seldom much left to chew from these. We had more luck with the rubbish bins. Late at night we would tour the streets with Kua leading the way, sniffing each bin and whining if there was any food inside worth pulling out. These hunts kept us fed for a while, indeed we often gathered more tucker than we could eat; until . . . the whites found out where we were getting our food and fitted each bin with a new heavy metal lid. With the help of the children I could just slide it down and we made more raids, but were now so slow that the darkness gave us time only to find a few scraps to keep us alive.

A man in uniform called early one morning and took Kua away — someone may have complained about him living with us or perhaps . . . The whites would hate to see a dingo sniffing their rubbish bins. We could not bear to be parted and sat outside the Dog Pound. Behind the thick wire-mesh fence, backed into a corner, Kua was seen facing a pack of snarling mongrels — if there had been time he would have climbed the fence, for a dingo like a possum cannot be enclosed unless within a cage. The children yelled and beat at the wire but I calmed them — whatever happens you must never raise your voice so that the whites notice you. But instead of being silent the kids made an even louder racket and a man in uniform rushed from his hut, red-faced and bristling like the angry dogs.

"Cut that out. Stop that barbarous noise. I've got beasts of my own yelling in here!" he shouted.

"We want our dog back."

"That cur! I just dumped it in there so the other dogs could have a snack."

"You stole it from us."

"It's never been vaccinated, no license fees have ever been paid, and you've bought no food for it. This is town, you know, not the bush."

Night fell, the mongrels stopped their howling, and Pingal, the Moon, sneaked out from behind a cloud to light the Pound. Kua jumped suddenly, scrambled over the fence and followed his shining ancestor out of the enclosure. No white man — no dog — saw him go.

A large white man's settlement sunk in a haze of dust lay spread on both banks of the dry river; it looked as though it had seen no rain for years. We dug a pit in the dry riverbed, warm and soft to rest in, but with

34

edges so powdery they slid suddenly and almost smoth-
ered the dingo. Poor Kua was terrified. He must have
thought it was a trap and refused to come back into the
hollow again, though I coaxed and called to him. It was
too cold for the children to sleep out on the sand so it
seemed as though we were to part, but Kua had other
plans.

He dug a burrow — tunneled deep into the steep
riverbank; a comfortable dugout with room enough for
us all and with, at its farther end, a hole, so narrow we
could scarcely squeeze through. Thus, should any danger
threaten at the main entrance, escape was still possible
— a dingo seldom will allow himself to be trapped.
Still, what comfort can the snuggest dugout, hut or
home bring when there is no tucker around?

There is usually a living to be found for a dog that
will work on a station property or for the police, but who
will trust a dingo to muster stock or track a thief? Kua,
however, had other talents and every day he went to
town and danced in the park, around the pubs and
wherever he saw the white men gather. He was very
good at the *gungi*, the rainmaking ceremony. None of
us could help much, and he had to do it all himself —
rearing on his back legs and, as he danced, knocking
the claws of his front paws together to make the sound
of clapping sticks. It was not possible for him to play
the *didjeridu*, so he made growling noises sounding
much the same as that instrument.

The whites thought the *gungi* dance was very funny.
They laughed at Kua and threw him a bone or a sand-
wich and sometimes even a meat pie. In the whole

country there was no man, mortal or spirit, who could have danced the *gungi* better; and when a blackfellow dances just right then his voice and the sounds of the dance float up to the sky and wake Pingal. The Moon answers with splashing water — the louder you sing and dance the more rain will fall, and if you are very good, the whole country could be flooded.

The white men took Kua to welcome the busloads of visiting tourists with his dance, and drove him to the airport to entertain the travelers; he demonstrated his dancing on T.V. — and the audience cheered and clapped but Kua was worried. He had so often called for rain, day after day, that when Pingal answered and splashed down the water there would surely be such a flood as had never been seen before.

We had to leave the burrow in a hurry. Kua had howled the whole night calling to me and the children to come out — luckily for us. Heavy rain had fallen high in the hills and a huge wall of water rolled down the riverbed tearing at the dry banks and sweeping away bridges. There was a great gum tree close by and the children climbed quickly into its branches. I scrambled up too, but poor Kua was struggling to cling to the tough trunk and the current, already swift, was sweeping him away. I took off my blouse and hung it quickly down, Kua gripped it in his strong jaws and we dragged him up.

The whites were busy fighting to save their own kind and none came looking for us till a day later, when the water had begun to go down. A boat came toward us with two policemen rowing breathlessly against the current. Behind them, on a tea chest, sat a bearded man wearing shining spectacles — the Do-Gooder at last, I thought.

"Hey! You! Lower that dog down here," ordered one of the policemen while the other tried to tie the boat to the tree trunk.

"It's good that you came, we would have starved."

"We're only concerned about that dog. Let it down."

Kua clung against the tree trunk quivering with fear. One of the policemen tried to climb up the tree and was almost halfway up when he suddenly slipped.

"We've gotta have that dog," yelled his mate. "It's a case of emergency. Most of the country is still under terrible drought. Stock are dying, men are starving!"

The men in uniform were growing angry. One of them threw a lasso; the ring of rope tightened around Kua's neck and a moment later he was pulled down into the boat and fastened in a cage.

"Let him go, he is ours," the children cried.

"It won't be for long," said the bearded man. "We only need to record his magic rainmaking code and program it on the computer. No harm will be done. All mankind will be grateful."

The two policemen rowed away toward the town. The boat moved quickly in the current and the bearded man sat on the tea chest smiling back at us.

37

The Miringu

THE JOURNEY must be nearing an end — a dead melaleuca tree shows itself against the sunset and the spears of its dry branches are black against the red clouds. I wonder if this really is Gopopingu, my *jiritja* country, or . . . but no, I could not have wandered anywhere else. When they let you out of jail they don't give you a ride home, but I would beat my way back, even if I had to go farther on — to Bralgu to join Wudal and the rest of our ancestors. For all these years I have dreaded the whites' keeping me till the very end and having to finish in a ditch or an incinerator.

I won't make a campfire; it would be hard to find sticks of the right wood to rub together to make the first spark and even if I got it started there is not much wood around to keep it going. A few skeletons of dead trees, that's all that can be seen from here to the horizon. It's not that I'm worried about the smoke giving me away — it has to come to that, sooner or later. The men of the Riratj clan must have already heard that I'm on my way back — a party with spears is probably already out in the bush to get me. They call it *miringu*; all the local tribes do, but the white man has a different word for it — revenge.

Better not to think of the *miringu* men. The birds — Dodoro, the pigeon, and Diridi, the hawk — have just come to rest on an uprooted tree stump for want of a better roosting place. Dodoro flits restlessly between the splinters of twisted root and cheeps incessantly; but even if he should cry the whole night he could not make a tree, or even a shrub. The ancestors could do it; during the Dreamtime they made the whole Gopopingu country and covered it with huge paperbark trees so tall they almost tickled the soft belly of the clouds. When last I was here this whole swampy plain was covered with them, but trees, rocks and even billabongs exist only until the whites come around grabbing. Perhaps Diridi understands that. He keeps his eyes closed most of the time, only now and then partly opening one eyelid to see if I am still around. He reminds me of a tribal elder, serene and calm . . . no matter how wildly around him rages the storm, he is always sure he will not drift away from the path to Bralgu.

The birds have been traveling with me for weeks now,

since the day I came from the jail. They weren't waiting at the prison gate — they're not birds you'd see flying in the town — but they came to me at the first camp and have stuck with me ever since. It's good to have someone — after all those years in a cell, you begin to think there is nothing, apart from four walls, close to you. Even the ancestors did not call often, and Wudal . . . but he's not to blame. The people from Bralgu, the land of our spirits, don't go peeping in the white man's jail, and to be fair, things have gone so badly here and surely no better in Ngaimil, my *dua* country, that Wudal was needed everywhere. Every black soul, tree or animal must have cried out for him. The whole country is naked; look, as far as the eyes take you the earth is nothing but monsoon-washed sand. Here not even the dead trees are left. Lucky I got up early this morning; the sun is not high yet and I can still move on, but by noon the heat will knock me to the ground. My good friend Dodoro woke me at dawn with his cooing and gave me no peace until we set off. Perhaps the birds knew what was to come and hurried me that this ugly stretch of country should be crossed before the sand heats up. I should try and talk to them. They could probably tell me how long I have before the Riratj mob will be here with their spears. I might learn from the birds why the whites decided to let me go home; though it might do me no good to know, I'd feel easier if I knew what the whites were up to. When they locked me in jail they said I'd be staying for the rest of my life, but scarcely half of that can have passed yet. Maybe the whites got tired of it all — letting me out of my cell to walk in the wire-fenced compound and locking me back between the walls again; or perhaps they didn't like the shouts of the white prisoners — "Bloody Bong, you never had it better in your life," and then, even louder: "Send the black bastard back to be speared!" I have no way of knowing what made them think differently but . . . the chaplain took me to the gate, a few weeks ago, and said: "Look, fella, we can't burden our consciences with you any longer. Go back and let your people be the judge."

I'll stretch on the ground here though the sand is hot like the ashes of a campfire. A huge caterpillar track from an abandoned bulldozer is half buried in the sand and its small arch casts a patch of shade, just big enough to shelter my head from the sun. The birds dive down to rest too but the moment their claws touch the burning metal they flap quickly back into the air with cries of protest. They don't try to alight again, but spiral upward to ride on the hot wind.

I passed here often with my mother when we traveled from Ngaimil to her maiden country; four camps — a long journey but we scarcely needed to come out into the sun for all the way we had the shade of the paperbark trees. High up in the branches the pigeons cooed endlessly, but we never speared any of them, or even searched for eggs in the hollow trees — you don't eat your *jiritja* totem, just as you never harm a close relative. There was plenty of other bush tucker to be found — just off the track stretched a great billabong almost hidden under a green cover of floating lily leaves. We never passed without splashing in to swim and gather the sweet flowers for a meal. The billabong . . . it was just over there, but only dry sand remains of it now and partly buried in that sand are the huge tires and rusting metal blocks of a giant scraper. It looks as though some terrible force had tossed the machine high up, then flung the scattered pieces back to earth.

I should not hurry so; the birds are suffering. Diridi's wings strike stiffly at the air like two palm fronds and he flies only a spear's length above my head. It should not be far, now, to Coromuru, the tidal river crossing, and if we need to wait there for low tide we'll have a spell at last. When I traveled with my mother, we often stayed for half a day, speared many fish in the water and had time enough to cook them in hot ashes. I will spear some again, for me, Diridi and . . . but Dodoro might not like such meat — the bush berries and seeds growing on the riverbank will be the right tucker for him.

If the Riratj mob is out for me they will be there — when *miringu* men are after someone, in the whole country there is no better place to wait than at the Coromuru Crossing. I wonder how many spears Riratj can muster for *miringu*; but they mightn't have spears at all, and come with guns. That mob likes to do things the white man's way. Since the first boat arrived, years ago, and stopped in the Bay at the mouth of the Coromuru, Riratj men have been hanging around the whites' camps for a handful of biscuits, an ax, or just

42

a red cloth. That mob! They'd give the whole country away for a single packet of tobacco. Anyhow, whatever they might have mustered — spears or guns — it can't be more than a few. Since learning the white man's ways meant discovering grog, the Riratj mob drank until their minds or their bodies rotted.

No, there's no *miringu* party around — windblown sand has nearly buried the charcoal of the old fires. It must be years since the last traveler crossed the Coromuru. On the bank there is no track or print — even the animals have stopped coming here. My birds both dive quickly to drink, but without touching the water's surface swoop as quickly away to perch on a nearby rock covered with a grayish mass.

Coromuru is so strange. Instead of water a liquid thick with green slime and crushed with sulfur lies between its banks. A smell like that of a burst rotten turtle egg hangs in the air. Near the water's edge and covered with a layer of sludge is a pile of fish skeletons and turtle shells. A violet haze sits on the water's surface as though the mist was drifting from the Bay upriver when all wind had suddenly stopped.

High in the air the birds circle again and Dodoro's coo calls me to move on again. From here, you can see Ngaimil, my *dua* country. It is there, on the other side of the Bay where that line of mountains rises from the sea toward the horizon. A bit to the right, the Wawalag Sisters — two pillars of rock — should be seen, and tucked between them and the arm of the Bay is a level gully. In the Dreamtime Wudal was traveling through

43

Ngaimil country, then dry and waterless. He camped on the hillside and made a ceremony calling for rain, but he danced and sang so hard that part of the hill slid down from the cliff and made that level place.

The birds cry out suddenly, flap forcefully with their wings and beat upward. There is nothing around to frighten them so maybe . . . yes, it is just their way of warning me that we are crossing Riratj country at last. I doubt that the men will come out. The booze . . . yes, that's all they think of now, not *miringu*.

I speared one of their tribesmen, and an eye should go for an eye — that's the law of both tribes. Yet, it happened so long ago, and the Riratj mob thinks nowadays of how to hang on to the whites and when they'll wet their throats again with a handout bottle of booze.

What's happened to the Sisters? Half the cliff has gone leaving nothing but a sheer face of rock, from the peak right down to the base of the hill. They've taken one Sister away, and the other is most terribly scarred. Stripped away are the rocks showing the coiling wet hair clinging to her body in the downpour for which Wudal danced. On her shoulders, where her head once lay, stands an ugly steel tower. The half-wrecked thing leans to one side and outward over the abyss of the ravaged hill.

Scores of banyan trees put in the gully by Wudal during that rain grew wide, and sheltered the tribe from the sun and wind. When the whites came to build a deepwater port in the Bay below the gully and tried to drive us to the hills, not one of the Ngaimil people moved, but one morning the bulldozers roared in and swept the huts, the trees, everything before them. We snatched up our spears; Awara, Tio, Rayum, Oke, Cungu, Iarku, Tataman and Yangarin — all those cousins who are now in Bralgu — everyone stood ready to fight. I took on a dozer driver but the white man was shielded by a blackfellow seated right on the nose of the machine. I threw; but the poor Riratj bugger — drunk or stupid — didn't dodge.

The whites must have sweated here, all right — in place of the banyan trees stands an immense building of molded concrete: the ore-processing plant, to crush the rocks that the white man is so mad about. The incoming conveyer belt has rusted and fallen leaving a huge opening in the wall like the entrance to a cave. All is deep darkness, warning of the abyss behind which has swallowed a whole hill of our land. One spear is left, sharp against the sky — an empty flagpole on the main tower — and just below it, the building has cracked in two. There it is! That's the port! It can be seen through the gap in the collapsing building. It's nothing much to look at, only a pipe, as wide as a tunnel, running from the plant to the sea. Some support pillars must have rusted for the wonderful pipe lurches and its snout is plunged in the oily dark water.

The blackfellows must have gone long ago. No tribe could survive here; the animals have left and even the crabs are sunk in their mudholes never to come out again. I wonder if any of us will return here as a tree or a star. Perhaps the birds can tell. They're sitting over there on a dead mangrove tree — Diridi half asleep and Dodoro turning his head so he can look straight in both my eyes. He knows but has no words to tell me his secret.

We must get on the track again for the rest of our journey. It would have been easier to go straight to Bralgu without calling at the *dua* and *jiritja* country — but maybe Wudal wanted it that way.

The Tracker

I SHOULDN'T be in this at all; you track an animal or
a snake but not a man. White fella will never understand that — he's keen to hunt down even his own kind.

It must be weeks now since they got me to lead this
hunt; I'm no good at counting, but there have been so
many night stops I've already forgotten some of the
places we camped. We've almost crossed Dead Adder
People country, a dry waterless stretch, with the boiling
sun sitting on our heads all day. It doesn't bother me
so much; I'm good for weeks more of it, but the whites
behind me — the Sergeant, the stockman and that fella
in the dark glasses — are already fighting for every
breath they take. Another day or two walking will be the
finish of them.

I wish they'd cracked up already, then the hunt would be off — but no, good things don't come my way, so why even think about them. This time, though, it'll be bad luck for all of us. It'll finish us all off, and just for once the white man won't have his way.

"Whoa!" The Sergeant calls for a spell.

The whites have crowded in the shade of a tree, but I'd rather stay out in the sun than bunch up with that mob. The sun doesn't bother me. If you're born in this country, and your skin is dark, the sun is like the touch of a mother's hand.

"How soon before we get that bloody bastard? . . . Hey you, Abo," shouts the man in the dark glasses.

"He can't hear you," says the Sergeant.

"Seems he doesn't talk either."

"He mumbles a few native words now and then."

"Couldn't you find anyone better for the job?"

"He's never failed yet."

"What a queer bugger he is. How do you communicate with him?"

"Abos know what's expected from them."

"It's like a hound," says the stockman. "You point to the track, and away he goes."

They don't talk about why they're hunting the poor bloke; don't even say his name. They needn't bother to try and fool me — I know it's Malu. You don't have to track for long before you know who you're after. When you track an animal — even a lizard — you can always tell how good a catch it will be, if it's worth chasing, and which way it will run. If it's a man you're trailing, you can even judge if he'll be caught, and when. Yes, it

48

hurts you to know, but it's better to know beforehand, and have time to think about your man. The boys who've grown up in the settlement are no good in the bush — they gallop like bullocks, without thinking. Malu would have been caught the first day out if that mob had anyone but me on the job.

I wonder why they're hunting him — what harm could he've done? None of them talk about that so maybe there's nothing much to say. The white men have made strange rules called "law" and it's pretty hard to live by it. From the beginning of my memories I've dreamed of finding the spell to make me free from the rules, and be able to just go my own way. But find the strength to do that, now, and the whole world, sky and all, falls on you.

They won't catch him. I'll see to that. It'd be worse for Malu if the joker in the glasses got to him — he reminds me of a knife blade. He sleeps by the fire with his boots on and his gun by his hand. A few days ago I caught him staring at me while he cleaned his glasses, and it felt like a cut from a whip on my skin. I wouldn't like to be in his hands — he'd break a man in half for the fun of it — cold, without rage.

A line of shade follows the trees in the dry creek bed; the footprints are clear in the sand. Bare feet are best for walking. They'll carry you to the end of the country, and the white man can follow only till his boots wear out; that's not far, either, on this rocky ground. Thirst's the common enemy, though, for even if your legs would still carry you, a dry mouth nails you to the nearest shade, and then it's only hours before you're finished.

The whites are slowing up — all of them. Their footsteps are dull thuds on the stony ground.

"How much farther could that bastard have gone?" asks the man in the glasses.

"We're getting closer all the time. Can't be far off now."

"Better not be. This bloody country! I've just about had it."

The Sergeant is easy to fool; Malu is still moving well — long strides on a straight course. He must have found water, for he seems fresh for another go. A blackfella never dies of thirst — not in his own country. If you dig in the sand in a riverbed you'll come across a frog or two; spear his belly and water will splash out. It doesn't taste the best, but if you're on the run you're not too fussy.

I never thought Malu would be so good at getting away in the bush; it looks like he'll outwit this lot, easy.

He made a campfire there, at the bottom of the dry water hole, and you'd miss it even if you passed by just a few steps away. There's a jump of sandstone nearby — steep and quite high. Yes, he's climbed there; good boy — you never sleep close to the campfire when you're on the run.

He's run out of matches by the looks — making fire the hard way now, with sticks. Bit of a job for a settlement boy — they don't get much practice at the old ways down there. But I taught him that trick a long time ago, and he shouldn't have forgotten it; he ought to remember how to hold the stick between his palms, straight and true against the wood below, and not to let it swing right or left. Fool, he hasn't bothered to smooth the stick and you can't slide your palms down the stick as you spin it if you leave it rough. He made a fire all right, but he'll have two handfuls of blisters, for sure.

He was a small boy when I taught him the way to make fire; we went walkabout together through the Dead Adder People country and made a camp somewhere near here . . . no, it would be farther up the creek, closer to the hills. That was before the white man came and made the first house down in the gully. We had no matches then.

"I just want to get him, and collect that bloody reward," says Glasses.

"Those Abos, they're as clever as dingoes in country like this," offers the stockman by way of excuse. "Look here, he's had a cockatoo for his tucker."

"That's the leg of a lizard, not a bird."

They're both wrong — that's a frog's leg. Malu's had food and water from the owner of that leg, so he's doing all right.

The whites are arguing noisily again. It's much better when they're quiet, and I can close my eyes and imagine I'm alone in the bush with the animals and the birds — they do no harm to mankind. If I keep my eyes closed, like that, for long enough my mind goes back and back. I can even sometimes hear the bull-roarer calling me from the far Dreaming. A few days ago — no, yesterday — I saw myself dancing at the water hole in the hills. All the Dead Adder People were there, the old men and the young blokes, and we danced so hard that a cloud of dust rose up and blotted out the sun till it was dark in the middle of the day. It was good to see my old mates — all of them gone long ago. They disappeared like the stars in the morning sky — it's hard to remember what happened to each one. But now and then you bump into a wandering spirit and it reminds you that all of us belong to the Dead Adder family.

The white men are trying to hurry me along, but I don't like being bullied. They'll know soon enough that it doesn't matter which way we go, or how fast, because the end of the road is very close.

I would like to see myself dancing again, but the picture doesn't come easily. Lately when I close my eyes the men come only one by one. There are so many of them, one after another, but each one alone. I don't remember tracking so many, but it must be right — the spirits always tell the truth. It'll be good to tell them that my turn has come, and I'm coming — and not only me, but the other too.

I can slow down here; we're climbing up a steep, rocky slope. There's not a tree in sight and the sun sits on your forehead like a rock pulled out of the hot ashes.

There's still quite a way to go; white men have too much to live for to crack up easily, and these are still talking about the reward to take their minds off the boiling sun. How big is the reward for Malu, I wonder. It must be sizable to take the hunters so far and so fast.

"I'll blow all my cut on beer," dreams the stockman. "It'd make a whole pool of booze you could swim in."

The others are silent. Their mouths must be dry and it's hard to get the words out.

We're not following the tracks any longer, but the boss men haven't noticed — they're so sure I won't go wrong. We're closer to the hills now — you can see a scattering of trees among the boulders. They'll go mad, those white men, when they know there's no way back. The sunglasses one — he'll probably use that gun. But it doesn't matter to me, now. There's nothing left for me at the settlement where all the Dead Adder People are just a handful of old women; all the men have gone, one by one. When you track for the white man, the blackfella gets caught, or he runs away — either way he's gone. They shouldn't have made me track Malu — even a dingo doesn't hunt his own breed; but white men . . . they've got no such pride.

There's not a sign of a breeze in the air; it gets pretty hot among these rocks, and even in the shade the ground is hot enough to roast a man. It must be about noon — the sun is high and cruel. By sundown everything should be over. That's the best way, and I won't have to face the old women at the settlement. Every time, before, when I've come back from a white man's job like this they've stared, hating me; cursing me without words, shouting bad things with their terrible eyes. It knocks you down like a blow from a *cunda* stick. The children throw rocks at me and call, "Cut-Cut, Bad Spirit." They run and hide if I come near — but chant and shout, following at a safe distance wherever I go.

It's good not to have to go back: the whites have

almost had it, now. They don't talk anymore, and stay lying on the ground. A little while ago they had quite a brawl, yelling and shouting till I thought they'd start shooting at each other or at me. I couldn't catch all they were saying, and it probably wouldn't have made sense to me anyway, but a lot of it was about rewards. The sun must have caught hold of their minds, or maybe it's the thirst.

They thought they had the reward here: a whole heap of money here among the rocks. The Sergeant and the man in the glasses were grabbing all they could — I never saw such a sight; the pair of them snatching at nothing and scraping their fingers on the rocks and rough sand as they crammed it in their pockets and inside their shirts. The stockman tried to take a share. They shoved him away, but he got angry and forced his way to the spot on the ground. The other two kicked at him and threw him backward. He rolled over like a bundle of grass in the wind and lay still, so they must have hurt him quite bad.

The two white men were happy for a while, with their pockets and shirtfronts full of rocks and sand. Then, though the weight of their "reward" dragged them to the ground, they crawled away across the stones — maybe trying to escape with their treasure. But thirst is an even heavier load than rock, and it tied them there on the hillside. Their mouths had dried long before, and their lips were scarred with bloody cracks. They moved only a few feet away and then scraped holes to dump and hide the muck from their pockets and shirts. Suddenly the hate and mistrust between them flamed up, and they turned to face each other, snarling like dingoes, before throwing themselves into battle, each one reaching for the throat of the other.

The stockman raised his head, but made no move to try and stop the fight. From where he lay just a few feet away came choking laughter: "Fighting over money . . . the treasures of all the world, and it can't buy peace, even here." He rolled on his back and kicked his heels in the dust as he laughed and laughed . . .

Now they're all lying still; the shade of the tree has moved away, but none of them has noticed. I could easily walk away, now. Behind that rocky ridge there's a deep water hole, well hidden between two boulders. It's the sacred water hole of the Dead Adder People; when anyone of us dies, the spirit goes to rest at the bottom of that hole, waiting to come to life again. All of my people are reborn, not as men, but as trees or birds or stars. If I can be born a dingo, no white man will ever catch me.

Malu must have passed the sacred water hole by now — he knows the water hole is there. I showed it to him when I taught him about the sacred places of our people; just as he will teach his son when the time comes, and that boy, his son. That's the way it will be as long as the black man lives in this country, and one day when we are all animals and birds, we'll meet at that water hole to drink. Deep between those boulders the white man will never find us.

Buwad, the Fly

THIS ROOM is like a box. It has no door or window and the area within the concrete walls is filled with semi-darkness. The stale air in here smells of damp earth and the acid of wine. It's hard to breathe this air which doesn't feel like air. It's more like the pressing of earth, of a landslide on my chest — the whites never told me jail would be like this.

There must be a door, or they couldn't have dumped me in; but I can't find one. No windows either. High up, close to the ceiling, is a small hole — a pigeon would hardly squeeze through it — and that throws just a handful of light inside. Not enough to tell you the time of day, though, or what the weather is outside. Still, it's something to know whether it's day or night.

I don't know why they box me in; the whites never tell you that. Even if I did know, it'd be no use to me. I never should have come from the bush; my grandfather is there still, deep in the reserve. "Don't go town; it's like an anthill. The big white mob — they eat each other." He was right, I shouldn't have come here. The whites aren't happy to see you around, and once you get in someone's way, or tread on a few toes, they lock you up just to keep you out of their sight. Maybe this is the best way for all of us and . . . well, there's not long to go now. I tried to explain it to my mother, and I wish she had understood me. Since they put me in, she's been here often, in my dreams nagging all the time. She has a friend, a white fella; he's a good lawyer and could get me out of this box — she would pay him well. The others, they'd all help — the policeman, the judge . . . she knows the lot, the whole town. She's done favors for all the men, whenever they felt like it.

Why should she bother about me? In twenty years, my whole life, I've seen her only once. I could never imagine how she looked, before, but now when she comes in my dreams she seems very young. She has a tiny waist and sharp breasts springing out like spears. She should stay away. I was only a few weeks old, a handful of cries and tears when she gave me to the old people — to grow up with them in the bush. It was better that way. There in the bush you don't get sweets and coddling but there is air to breathe and space to run. If she'd kept me here in this ant heap . . . no, I wouldn't have grown up at all.

I wish my grandfather would come. I'd be happy to

see him — he could help me to get out of here — he knows about that sort of thing. I wonder why he hasn't come. I haven't seen him for . . . ten years — even more. He could be already gone, I suppose, and . . . that will be it! He'll come from the Dreaming. But the spirit world is far away and it's taking him a long time on the journey. But he will come; he'll get me out.

The concrete walls around me look like solid rock. Apart from that pigeonhole there's not a single crack, not a hair's breadth of a gap to let in any light. There must be some secret door, some channel to the outside world, because, now and then, I hear people talking and moving — even see them sometimes. There, outside, sitting in the sun with his back to the wall, is my cousin Katungal. He's only a couple of years older than I, but he coughs and retches like an old man; some evil must have caught him and he sounds as if he can't fight it for long.

A white man with a briefcase comes smiling to Katungal, puts the case on the ground, and pulls out a great bottle of methylated spirits. My cousin reaches for the grog with two hands, but that whitey is quick to snatch the bottle back and holds out a piece of paper instead. "Don't sign it," I yell. "The whitey's tricking you." I wish he could hear me. That paper's about our tribal land — you sign and the land is gone. The white man will clear the bush, and mine the rock.

Katungal looks blank; he can't sign — he doesn't know a single letter. The white visitor pats him on the shoulder. "Wait a minute, my friend," he says and hurries away. "You fool, don't let him trick you," I scream — I'm beating my fists against the concrete wall. Katungal makes no move; he doesn't hear me. Maybe if I shout louder I can make him listen: the white men will move in tomorrow, level the sacred water hole and cut the trees. They will dig deep to quarry the ore and the whole country will be an ugly, bare desert of dust.

I'm sorry about Katungal — and about myself too. When we were boys in the bush Katungal taught me to throw a spear and to set a fish trap. I've forgotten most of what I learned, but if I ever get out of here I'll head for the bush again, and I could use my cousin's help.

That white man's back, smiling slyly, and he's brought a lawyer, a policeman and a man with a camera — all bright-faced fellas. Still Katungal can't sign; but that doesn't matter now the mob of whites are there as witnesses. They show the blackfella how to make a cross and that's good enough. The camera clicks and the whole world will be able to see my cousin Katungal with the pencil in his hand.

The whites are leaving, but the show's not over yet. Katungal shouts after them and his voice is loud and angry. The smiling man understands the yelling, and quickly turns to chuck him the bottle of metho.

These walls are solid and firm — you could kill yourself calling for help, but no one would hear. Only my grandfather could show me the way out; he knows how the whole world of the blackfella is made, and how the animals and the trees came to life. I don't know why, but since I've been here, trapped by these walls, I think often about our ancestor Buwad. My grandfather talked of him often, a long time ago. During the Dreamtime,

Buwad, the Fly Man, lived in our country where the fish
and yams were so plentiful he could spend nearly all
his time singing and dancing. One day the Bad Spirit
Waruk came to the country and took all the tucker for
himself. Buwad was allowed only the scraps, and had to
beg for those. Whenever he came for food, Waruk
would chase him away, but Buwad had nowhere to go
and kept coming back to beg again. Presently Waruk
invited Buwad to feast on a great heap of fish in his
cave and when Buwad was inside rolled a boulder
across the entrance. But Buwad wouldn't be trapped —
he changed himself into a fly, and a tiny crack was big
enough for his escape. He's still a fly, and whenever he
smells food he comes begging and buzzing for his share.

I wish I could sleep; then the time would pass faster,
and I might wake up already changed into an insect —
a fly maybe or anything small enough to squeeze
through that pigeonhole. But when I close my eyes I see
Wudlaru; she sits in a shelter made from two sheets of
rusty corrugated iron. She's skinny and her dress . . .
no, just scraps of rag the color of dust and smoke, flap
as if they're hung on a stump, not worn by the body
of a woman. She limps, my Wudlaru, from a wound
she's tied up with newspaper and string to keep out the
flies. A baby's crying, crying without stopping. It's
lying wrapped in rags at Wudlaru's feet, and I can't see
it clearly. Two other children, naked half-castes, sit in
front of the shelter grubbing through a heap of rubbish.
The place must stink, but I expect the brats are used to
that — they don't seem to notice. Their faces are clotted

with swarms of flies, but they hardly bother to brush them away.

One child runs to the mother with bread he's found on the filthy heap and Wudlaru crumbles it for the baby — but the crying doesn't stop.

We were married years ago, then lost each other — some power was forcing us apart all the time. We both tried hard, but we couldn't live together. I wish I could say something to her now, or even just smile. It'd be good to sit down together and talk; I might cheer her up a bit. I'm not angry that the children are half-caste; I'd even look after them — have them live with us, maybe.

It must be night, now; there's no light from the pigeonhole any longer. It's worse than in that cave. My legs are growing stiff and I have to get up and walk about, now and then. If you are a bushman you are on the move all the time and stay on your feet as long as you are alive.

The darkness is thick here, and wherever I turn I'm face to face with a concrete wall. It was very bad in the beginning, when I screamed, and cursed the whites for building a box not big enough for an animal.

No, the walls don't upset me any longer; I've learned to walk in a small circle — round and round. I'm so used to it I can move like that for days, and feel I'm traveling far across the country. In the dark around me I see the trees and the scattered boulders, and I can hear the wind in the leaves. Sometimes I hear birds, and bees buzzing in the blossom.

After such a long journey round and round, you grow dizzy, and when I stop I'm as exhausted as a man returned from the hunt.

Grandfather should be here by now. It's so long since they locked me in that I've almost forgotten what it's like outside. Maybe my grandfather is angry with me, and won't come after all. No, he's not like that — he'll help me to find a way back to our country. He's in no hurry, of course, so that I stay here, in trouble, long enough to remember it well. Then, when I'm changed into a fly, or a bird or an animal, I'll never leave the bush again.

What will I become, I wonder; a bird would be good, but it's not for me to decide. Wiringan, the powerful spirit-man from the Dreamtime, will make the decision and tell me what he wishes. He will make me into a fly, maybe, but I won't mind. I'm not sure how this changing business works — if I'd stayed a bit longer on the Reserve the Old Men would have taught me. There might be some words to say or sing that would hurry it all up; I must point all my thoughts at Wiringan. But I needn't worry — Grandfather will tell me what to do. He won't leave me to manage alone and maybe make a mess of it.

It could be . . . yes, Grandfather is busy helping Katungal. I see him struggling through the mangroves, sinking knee-deep in the mud at every step. The tangled roots and branches catch at him like barbed wire and his face is a mass of scratches and wounds. Blood and sweat, mixed, runs down and drops red in the mud.

He's not far ahead of the tracking party and their

howling pack; the animals are excited by intermittent pistol shots. A helicopter circles overhead to direct the hunting party after their man.

That's where Grandfather will be for sure. It won't take him long to finish there — Katungal is already stuck in the swamp and the white men are closing in. Soon the hunt will be over and Grandfather will come to help me. In a few hours — before the dawn — I will be a fly. I'll dart out through that pigeonhole, rise high up in the air, and head straight to my people.

Girigiri, the Trap

I OFTEN WONDER why white men are so mad on rocks. When he dies each of them gets nothing more than a stone hardly big enough on which to chisel his name, yet during a lifetime, many of them have destroyed whole mountains.

There's that horrible rattling noise again. It's like a snake hidden in the scrub only a step or two away; you know it can kill you, but you can't see it. The machine must still be far away, though, for no matter how hard you gaze into distance, there's nothing to be seen yet but the blank horizon. Suddenly, there on the mainland, a dark ball appears in the air. It looks as though it had jumped up from the gray barren hills of mining waste. It floats uncertainly in the air for a while and then, in a curve like a thrown spear, heads this way across the sea. When it reaches the island shore the machine disappears from view, hidden for a while behind the sand dunes. But the sound is still there, hammering in the air more vigorously than before. It's here — the 'copter has appeared quite suddenly above the dry branches of a ghost gum and with the lust of a hawk diving on its quarry drops to the earth. From the dry bed of the billabong dust rises in a cloud and the dead trunk of an old paperbark tree crashes under the force of the man-made wind.

I don't like that man, the Prospector. He reminds me of Mamandi, the Bad Spirit. He's in no hurry to get out of the 'copter; the dust in the air is already falling back to the ground and he's still in the cabin; still in his seat. Maybe I'm expected to rush to him with the bag of rocks, bow down in front of the 'copter, and point the way to an island where he can dig whole hills of uranium. The Prospector stares at me . . . he looks at me as though I'm not a man but a cyclone which has just wiped out his whole fortune.

The cabin door opens a little; enough only for the voice to reach me:

"Where're the rest of you?"

"Missus and the boy are up in the bush."

"I didn't see them from the air."

"Could be under the rock shelter, just stop for a little rest."

"What about the instrument — the Geiger?"

"Gudjuringu, my wife, has it. They're looking for rocks."

What a bastard, this white man, who likes neither my voice nor my color, yet wants *me* to come up with a miracle that will make him a god. I shouldn't have got myself into this, but . . . what can you do? When you're black, no one asks you how you want your own life to be led.

The night before the Prospector flew us to Girigiri, the island here, to look for rocks I had a dream — Wudal, our ancestor from the Dreaming, called on me. I had never seen him before, but a long time ago, when I was a boy, the elders, the Gunavidji men, taught me many songs about him. He looked mighty indeed, with a stone ax tucked at the waist behind his *bongaru*, the belt made of human hair. His spear was hooked on a *mangal*, a spear-thrower, ready to charge. "They have found our *bad-maraiin*; don't let them get away with it!" I don't know what I could have done. *Bad-maraiin*, a rock and the most sacred of our totems, had been in a museum for years, and for the whites it was hardly worth a glance till, not long ago, a fellow in jail read me from the paper that in galleries and museums interest had grown. The whites were peeping with their electronic gear into our stone axes, spears and clay-painted figures for any traces of uranium. The white man has gone crazy on minerals lately, but it's not fair to stick your nose into the sacred secrets of someone else's belief. The last time they put me in the lockup it was only for sheltering on a church doorstep during a night storm. They kept me in jail for a week, but it could have been for a year if the Prospector had not bailed me out and then led me to his 'copter. Perhaps,

66

this is just as bad, maybe even worse than being in jail, but what could I have done? Before he pushed me in, I saw that Gudjuringu and the boy were already inside the 'copter.

"You'd better shape up soon," said Prospector now. "There'll be no tucker or water until I get those rocks . . . and . . . I won't be coming over again for a while."

Like a huge bull-roarer, the blade of the helicopter spins and the dust rises again. Up it goes, the metallic sound blending with the whistling of the wind till it fades away over the mainland into the vastness.

It will be days before the 'copter is back again; I hope Gudjuringu can hold on until then without proper water and tucker. Poor girl, she's been taking it hard, crawling over the sand and staring out to sea. I tried this morning to get her some oysters. There, just off the beach, the sea rocks are covered with them. I spent hours in the water and gathered a great heap, and yet — every single shell turned out to be empty. There's not much life left around; the sea creatures have sunk deep in the sand never to appear again. No hermit crabs crawl along the water's edge any longer, and even the sand flies have vanished.

Gudjuringu; she knows that there's not much still to hope for. I left her in the shade of *badbad*, those huge boulders down at the beach, there where the sea forms a small inlet. Once, it used to be . . . our ground for *kunapipi*, that the whites call the fertility ceremony. At the right time of the year the whole Gunavidji mob gathered there, and we, the young ones, had our bodies painted all over with the white, yellow and red clay. The

67

elders wore the ceremonial *djamar*, the headdress made of white cockatoo feathers, and the dance lasted for a whole day until the following night when all of us, even the children and women, rushed to the billabong for a communal bath.

The animals liked that inlet too; tortoises crawled often from the water and laid their eggs in the sand at the edge of the dunes, but nothing of it remains. In the valley around the inlet grew thick mangroves full of the calls of animals and birds. It's strange now; the trees are like bones; not a single leaf to be seen. I wonder, was it poison in the air or in the water of the rising and falling tide that murdered everything it touched. It must be both, because not only the inlet but the whole island looks like a skinned carcass.

Look, Gudjuringu is gone. She was sitting right here. I had brought her some seawater in a *womara* — the shell of a dead tortoise — to wet her skin. She's used all the water; the shell's here and the ground around it's still wet — she can't have gone very far, and the boy must have walked with her. He was sitting there, against the trunk of that casuarina tree, just above the rocks. I'd made him a fishing rod; wrecked that bloody Geiger and pulled the guts out of it. There was enough wire there to stretch a line as far as Bralgu — but no good came of it. The sea is just as empty as the island and anyway you couldn't find a single insect to use as bait. Still, the rod kept the boy busy and helped him forget his thirst for a while.

Has she gone into the sea? No, Gudjuringu never was a fool and I've known her from a little child. Yes, I was going to school when she was born. Over there on the mainland, close to the beach, we used to sit on the sand under a banyan tree. There's nothing of it to be seen now though. That tree was the first to fall when the whites arrived to build the mine. None of us ever did learn anything in that school, you know. The teacher was a missionary — Barndja, the white clay, we called him — and he was the first white man we'd ever seen. He kept a long stick in his hand and wrote with it in the sand under the banyan tree. Large letters he wrote: C-H-R-I-S-T, and we were asked to repeat first each letter and then the whole word. C-H-R-I-S-T was the only word we learned. Maybe there should have been something more but Barndja never did get around to it. He was too busy with his Geiger counter. *Nauaran*, the snake, we called it because of the long cord and black rod at its end. With it hung from his shoulder, Barndja would walk miles through the bush poking the rod here and there into the ground and then waiting breathlessly to hear it tell him that at last he had located the rock for which he lusted. We hadn't even learned the proper spelling of C-H-R-I-S-T before Barndja packed all his rocks into a bag and left for town in a hurry.

I could see no footprints on the sand; not Gudjuringu's, or the boy's. Where did they go? Whichever way they headed the footmarks should be left behind. I'm good at "reading" tracks. You can tell from his footprints how far the traveler will be able to go and if he is sick, angry or happy and not only from blackfellow tracks but the white man's too.

We always thought Barndja would come back one day

carrying his *nauaran* machine. There on the mainland was a whole mountain of rocks; enough to keep him busily poking with that rod for the rest of his life; in the whole world there could be no better place to keep him happy. Yet, instead of Barndja a column of bulldozers came crawling with an awful roar and smoke. Not one of us, I'll bet not even the mighty Wudal from Dreaming, knew what was happening. The whites stuck the ground with *marain* poles, surveyor's pegs they call them, and the caterpillars crawled on ripping the earth to dust.

The bulldozers will be back again should the Prospector have his luck. But if he ever finds uranium, it won't be here. He got it all wrong from the start. On this whole island, Girigiri, we call it, the rocks are sandy and soft. Those boulders down at the beach are a bit harder certainly, but they are different. They didn't come from the ground but were changed into rocks from tortoise eggs during the Dreamtime, when Wudal was around here. There's not a single stone on the island like those of the mainland hills that the whites blasted and dragged away; every Gunavidji man could tell you that, but all of them have gone to Bralgu and I'm the only one left.

Our *bad-maraiin*, that totem rock the whites put in the museum, didn't come from Girigiri. It was left to us by Wudal. What a fool, that Prospector. The Gunavidji are not islanders, they're the mainland mob, and it was only after the whites arrived and began eating the hills that we had to move away.

It does not look too far to the mainland — perhaps I

could swim across if I wasn't so worn down by thirst. There's nothing of use to be found there on the beach — the rusting steel skeletons of the sheds can be of no help. A few of the cranes still keep their heads above the ground though their bodies are swollen by the rising sand. Of the trucks and loaders only the tops can be seen and the rest is hidden in the dust — those machines might make a good nesting place for snakes should there be any left alive. Such a place would be of little help even to Mamandi. Maybe, though, if you moved farther inland, several camps away — there might be some country still left alive enough to support scrubs and reptiles.

At the right time, yes, I'll swim across. My father and some others did it, not long after we'd been driven here from the mainland, and they lit a fire to let us know they'd reached the other side. In the time before the white men came to Girigiri, the trap, it was a part of the mainland. It's an odd shape, three camps long and hardly two voices wide, and it lies alongside the mainland shore like the carcass of an eel with its tail plunged into the mainland. The land there was low and during high tide the water would rise in the mangroves and cut off Girigiri till the tide turned. We often would drive kangaroos and *djinabano*, the buffalo, from the mainland over the "tail" to the island and once the animals were trapped on the narrow shaft of land they could easily be speared. The same had happened to the Gunavidji people — when the whites came, they drove us across the "tail" into the trap.

Hold on . . . Look, there's a big hole where the sand

has been dug with a *djad*, a yam stick, and shoveled with hands — Gudjuringu and the boy have been here, do you see how clear their footmarks are? There are no tracks to show which way they came and where they went, but they were surely here not long ago for the digging is fresh. She should know that there's no water on Girigiri and you only waste your sweat looking for it. The only water we ever found was near the mangrove — it's a dry stump now — below the billabong, and even that didn't last the whole year. During the dry weather we would gather at the shore waiting for days before the missionaries would come from the mainland with a few barrels of water.

I'll stretch on the ground and rest for a while — my legs won't carry me for much longer. I wonder that Girigiri didn't float out to the open sea. Our ancestors told us that should you disturb the ground at the "tail," it might cut the island off the mainland, so we never dug for yabbies there for fear Girigiri would drift away like a dead eel. The whites didn't bother to take care though and, after we were driven from the mainland, their huge machines cleared the whole "tail" and set the island free. We thought it was all to keep us trapped, but no, they dug the "tail" away until the water was deep enough for the huge ships calling to take away rocks to pass through the strait.

It's quite a stretch of water from here to the mainland and the whites usually crossed in small boats though a few swam. They came mostly with grog, and often, for a bag of fresh water, won the prettiest girl in the tribe.

My father and the tribesmen who went across had

hoped to sneak behind the mining settlement and move deep inland in search of land for their people but I don't think they found any. If they did, they never came to tell us.

Night must have fallen some time ago, it's so cold. I should have made camp, there's enough dry wood around — there's been nothing green for years. There might still be some *duladna* too, the soft bark, to catch up the first spark. But I'm not good at making fire. I should be ashamed — it would take me the whole night and palms full of blisters to make a blaze.

No, it can't be a dream — the scent of the water is so strong in the air. There's no morning dew around — the sun is too high in the sky and the sea has never smelled this way before. Look, there's a whole pool full and water gushes up and threatens to overflow the banks. Yes, it's good and sweet: I haven't tasted anything fresh like this for weeks.

A shadow like a huge bird is passing over the sand — the Prospector is back. A gusty wind blows toward the mainland so loud and strong I can't hear my own voice let alone the 'copter. The machine hovers in the air while a steel rope winches down with a bag tied to its end. There could be food and water in it, but more likely there are tools and gear for chipping the rocks. The wind grows even nastier now, blowing sand in the air, and the Prospector tries to hold against it, but the 'copter begins to drift away. It's heading toward a gum skeleton and . . . it only just dodged around the branches. It's still drifting and . . . the machine suddenly seems to grasp for a grip on the air. The rope's caught on something; it's stretched to breaking point surely, but no . . . a chunk of wrecked caterpillar emerges from the sand, and the straining 'copter drags it away toward the mainland, until it hits the edge of the water . . . I can't see much through the sandstorm — the 'copter looks more like a floating shadow than a machine as it loses height and is swallowed by the sea.

The storm has died away but the dust haze still hangs in the air. Gudjuringu! Surely, it's she and the boy. She carries a *murga*, a dilly bag, and they are walking over the sea toward Bralgu. Wudal is leading them and his spear sways in the air as he steps over the waves. They haven't far to go; they're just about to step onto the rocks. I should call to them to wait for me, but no, I don't think they'd hear. Maybe . . . yes, I'll rest for a while until the dust settles, drink the sweet water once again, and then swim toward the mainland as my father did. I feel that's what Wudal would want me to do.

Goarang, the Anteater

THIS PLACE is like a trap; there is hardly a foot of room around me and whichever way I turn I come against wire mesh. They should have let me go, not because I don't belong to this strange place but because the whites usually get tired of keeping you in the lockup. There is nothing left for them to do so they let you out. After all, what's the point in having me here — you punish a native because he's a different color or because he has land you want to grab, but . . . once you grow to realize it's an anteater in your hand, not a human being, it's hardly fair to keep a harmless animal in jail.

Just once a day they open the cage to chuck in some food and water. You don't get bush tucker here. Instead

75

of a lizard or a handful of ants, you're given tinned slop;
what a vile smell it has — I can never be sure if it's
meant to feed you or finish you off.

There's a girl in white overalls . . . she's not here
now, but she'll be back — only slips away for a moment;
otherwise she's here in the room all day to keep an eye
on me. No, she's not like a policeman; she smiles now
and then, but she measures every bit of tucker and
water given to me and writes it in a book. She chats to
me often but . . . I don't like the way she calls me "Boy."
She strokes my back too, even though she's pricked her
hand many times on the spikes. The whites don't like
to be told they are wrong, but *she* should know that
although you are changed into an animal, or even an
insect, you retain your sex and — I could be her mother's
mother, almost twice over, in years.

The girl rushes in with a newspaper in her hand:
"Look, they've printed a photograph of you; what a
graceful pose, Boy . . . Lovely. And almost a half page
written about you. Listen: 'After many years of experi-
mental research Professor Tinto has successfully mini-
mized the shape of an unidentified Aborigine into an
echidna — a development which will undoubtedly en-
sure the survival of the Aboriginal race. Due to mining
expansion on their tribal land, the natives are on the
verge of extinction caused by severe lack of traditional
food and space. Thanks to Professor Tinto's discovery,
whole families or clans may survive on one handful of
ants and can be easily accommodated in a small cage,
sewer pipe or hollow log.' "

The whites can only see things the way it pleases

76

them. No professor but only the spirits of the ancestors from Bralgu could change a human into a bird, a star or a tree; we owe our lives to Wawalag, not to the white man. They might grab your land, kick you into the dust, and roar over you with bulldozers, but you will spring to life somewhere else. Think of these trees, animals and birds in the bush; they were all our people once, every one of them, but reborn. The whites . . . no, they'll never understand that. I often thought Gardagan, whom the whites call Rio Tinto, would have learned something of the way we are born. He should have, after all that time he spent in Ulaki, our tribal country. I would never have known his first name but for the girl here. I suppose that seems a bit odd — after knowing a man for years, gathering bush tucker for him, making up his campfire, and bearing him eight children — but what difference would it make to know his name. The Ulaki elders called him Gardagan, "one who wanders through the bush like a dingo."

Ulaki is a broad country; you need many camps to travel across it, yet Gardagan had sniffed through every valley and gorge, poked his nose into every grove, cave and billabong. There is hardly a plant the leaves or roots of which he did not gather and he had boxes full of insects, worms and beetles.

I was so shy that I never asked him what he was searching for — and days, even weeks might go by without me being brave enough to speak at all. I was given to him to make camp, gather tucker and . . . all the rest. Of course our country was then so vast that even a blackfellow would have trouble finding his way,

77

so someone needed to take care of Gardagan. The way a girl is told to go to an old man I was sent to him. Yes, it was meant to be a marriage; the Ulaki people saw it that way.

"Come on out, Boy — it's time to hop on the scale."

The girl drags me out of the cage again. I wish she'd stop nagging me. She does this three times a day and though there's already a whole book of figures written yet still she checks my weight again.

"You're doing fine, Boy, excellent. Professor Tinto will be pleased with you. Hop inside now — back into your sweet little home."

The Ulaki people first thought Gardagan was hoping to be eligible for the *maraiin*, the ceremony that would make him into a full man, and then to find a place of his own to settle. The elders didn't mind him coming to our country. Loaded aboard his small boat he always brought a heap of white man's tucker, tobacco and grog . . . the grog, of course. "What stuff!" the elders would say whenever they thought of that drink, later. Gardagan gave a pocketknife to each Ulaki man, and every woman in the tribe received a box of matches. For a month after that no one bothered with fire sticks. He spoke softly, almost pleadingly, and everyone thought a man like that couldn't even step on an ant. The people knew nothing of his passion to learn about the trees, the animals — everything that meant life to the Ulaki country. He had a small tent, and whenever we camped it would be pitched, not far from the fire, and there he would sort the leaves, the buds, the roots, the insects and . . . yes, the bits of rock gathered from here and there and tucked away in the bag.

Each year with the first rumblings of thunder and when the early showers announced the coming of the Wet, the young men from the tribe would be called. The camping gear, the instruments and all the gleanings from the bush were already packed and waiting in bags to be carried down from the plateau across the still drought-parched plain and over the dry billabongs and swamps ahead of the rain to the bank of the river. Every year it was so, as predictably as the arrival of the monsoon. And every year, just as predictably as each wet season subsided and not long after the last thunder was blown westward far beyond Ulaki country, the rattle of the engine would rise from the mouth of the river. The noise would echo in the branches of the banyan trees and shortly the small boat itself would come nosing at the edge of the mangroves.

"It's the time for your temperature check; come on, Boy. Where's that hidden spot?"

The girl plunges a thermometer into my back hole. She does it twice a day and perseveres with the job no matter how much I scream and fight.

"Smile, Boy, just a little smile for me. You looked so good on T.V. last night — with the whole world watching. Ouch! You pricked me. What a passionate lover you'd make."

The children, if they were still around . . . No, I don't think they'd recognize Gardagan. They hardly knew him and . . . what could they say to each other?

Gulwiri, the boy, had his father's big ears and something of his skin . . . not *so* light but halfway between
us. The baby was only a few weeks old when Gardagan
came back to the country and I had to leave him with
my mother to be cared for. The following year came
the twin girls, Ewinga and Nabiow, both with fair hair
but such dark eyes. My mother loved them, but the
other people from the tribe . . . they were eager to
tease and laugh. Next came Okundah, the strange boy,
who never cried. As he grew up he spoke no words.
Maybe there was nothing to say. After him came the
triplets — Coari and Irawala, the boys, and Djad, the
girl. So many people came peeping into the hut to see
them . . . but not Gardagan — I don't think he noticed
the children at all. On his comings and goings to Ulaki
country or to his boat on the river he would be always
watched by the children hidden behind tree trunks and
bushes, and waiting to pounce on a discarded cigarette
packet or the wrapping from a film. Gardagan seldom
turned to them and even if he had, he would not
recognize our children among the rest.

Erang was the last to come but . . . poor boy, he
never even made a cry. It was only a few days before
he should have been born when a fleet of barges
arrived upriver. From the metal belly of each ship
crawled a bulldozer — over the Settlement — over the
huts, smashing them to the ground. Those who could
run got away but . . . I was knocked down by falling
saplings and as I struggled in the ruins Erang was born
— dead.

The old people say there are so many Ulaki children

dying because they can't bear to stay alive and see what's happening to the tribe. Perhaps it's better that way; the earlier you go, the less time there is to cry. Once the bulldozers arrived most of the Ulaki country was quickly cleared; trees, scrub and even the soil was scraped away, leaving only rock. No place was left to dig yams, and for scores of camps around, no bird, kangaroo or lizard could be found. The children cried all night for tucker, and all we had for them was water. Irawala was one of the first to be silenced and with him many many Ulaki children who cried no more. Some kept themselves alive for a while begging around the mining camp or searching through the rubbish dump behind the white man's canteen. Coari, the other triplet boy, would climb about the machines during the night, and sniff the fuel in their tanks. The stuff would make you dizzy and sent you to the Dreaming for days . . . The boy liked it more and more, and at last the Dreaming claimed him forever. Poor Okundah; he wandered close to where the miners had set a charge and flew to the sky together with a whole hillside of rock. Gulwiri, better than any of them, had the sense to keep away and went often down to the river mouth to look among the rocks for oysters. The best place is just where the sewerage is pumped from the mining settlement and the water around it is greenish; some say it stinks, but Gulwiri didn't mind. The last time he went there he became sick and couldn't swim back from the rocks. When we went later to help him — it was too late; the tide had washed him away.

The girls? Oh yes, they've suffered too. The police

took me, one day, to see the body of a girl they'd found in the heap of empty tins and beer bottles in the bush behind the canteen. Yes, it was Nabiow. But I only knew by the pale hair. The other twin, Ewinga, was taken to hospital — they said she had some rotten sickness and had to be kept away from others. It's happened to other Ulaki girls before and once they're taken away to be cured they never come back to us again.

I am hoping Djad might have better luck. There was only a handful of the tribe left and because she was too young and frightened to wander on her own I had to look for tucker for both of us. Even though the ground bore no yams and the animals had fled the country we still had to live. The lucky ones were the birds. They could fly away to a better place.

These whites; they really are mean. They have hills of food piled up in their stores, and often dump whole truckloads of bread at the rubbish tip. One loaf was all I took from the shop and . . . the whites were very quick to drag me away to the lockup.

I wished Djad was with me in the jail; it would have been easier for us both. At night I often heard her voice coming through the bars as if she called from a misty distance. The call came night after night, no matter if outside it was storm, moonlight, rain or wind, but as the days went by and the seasons changed from Dry to Wet and back again, her calls faded away. I hope she's found the way to Bralgu at last.

"Wake up, now. Be a good boy. Look who's here — it's Professor Tinto come to show you to his students, so put on a nice face."

A big mob of young people stares at me; amazed, most of them — openmouthed. I hate being stared at as though these people are going to snatch me. I curl myself into a tight knot, face to belly, so all that remains of me is a ball of spines. The whites won't try to grab that. Out in the bush Goarang does that to save himself from danger; but the dingo — you can't fool him. He rolls the anteater over the ground to the nearest water hole; once Goarang stretches out to swim the dingo has him.

Gardagan pokes me in the back with a stick and says:

"This present form is only the transition stage of the Aboriginal being. In the further evolution of our idea we will reduce this form to the shape of an ant. Then it will be possible to feed a whole tribe with a single scrap of rotten garbage."

"Do you hear that, Boy? Professor Tinto is taking you with him to deliver his Governor Arthur of Tasmania Memorial Lecture."

Why can't they let me alone if they won't let me free in the bush to fend for myself? When I was first in jail, still in human shape, Gardagan used to come, only now and then, but later more and more often. That was many years after we had last seen each other in the Ulaki country and he gave no sign that he recognized me, but surely he did. Even if the face should fade from memory because it's black, the voice would still remain. I believed that he remembered me well, but said nothing because the prison guard was always listening outside the cell hoping for something to gossip about. Whites gossip both for gain and as a sport. I really believed that Gardagan was visiting me more and more often in the hope of a moment when we could be alone. I had to show him the children. Yes, all of them — Gulwiri, Ewinga, Nabiow, Okundah, Coari, Irawala, Djad and Erang — were up there in the sky every night, rising slowly from the mist near the Milky Way. You could hardly miss them as the first seven travel in a group like a flock of birds and leading Erang, not far behind, but harder to see.

It was a pity Gardagan came to my cell mostly in daylight and though he twice visited me at night each time the sky outside the small barred window was so cloudy that even the moon didn't show. The chance must come for me to show the man his children, or so I hoped and believed and lived only for that. That wish kept me alive for so long in spite of the white man's neglect, I hoped and waited for so many years that my hair grew gray and instead of living for that happy moment . . . I woke suddenly one night and felt . . . I was Goarang, the anteater, and not a woman any longer. The bars on the jail around me had grown smaller too, and had shrunk to the size of a cage.

The white mob has gone. Yes, now the door is locked, I can stretch myself safely again, and though there is not enough room to walk about I can move in a circle, close my eyes, and pretend I am in the bush. But no. Not all of them have left the room. I can hear noises and heavy breathing. Gardagan and the girl are still here. Their clothes are scattered on the floor and their naked bodies are pressing against each other but no words are spoken. When he's busy with a woman

Gardagan never talks, but he takes great choking breaths. It always reminded me of a snake fighting to swallow a pigeon.

It is far better to close the eyes; to pretend that you have crawled under a log in the bush and that around you rushes the sound of the wind caught in a hollow tree. Even if a dingo should come to sniff and roll you to the nearest billabong, it will be the end of the life you have been born for, and not one forced upon you.

Balanda Mob

THE MANHUNT must be coming to an end — there across the dry creek bed two *balanda* — white — men are dragging a third to the shade of a paperbark tree. Now and then I can see their faces showing red and sweaty above the scrub as they struggle toward some shelter from the sun. A blackfellow, the tracker, walks behind carrying a bag of water; as soon as they reach the tree a *balanda* grabs it and wets his throat in a great hurry and splashes water on his mate lying stretched on the ground.

They should know by now that I am *birimbir* — a spirit — and not a man any longer. It happened many camps ago. I was running when my *ganguman-ganguman* — my grandfather — appeared in front of

me: "Come to us to Bralgu, I will make you *margidju*
— a native doctor." The *balanda* mob should have
sensed, when they found my spear and wommera left
lying on ground, that I would have no further need to
fight or even to hunt, but they will not, cannot understand a thing which pleases them so little. They prefer
to think that I am growing breathless and will soon
give myself up, so they are rushing to get their hands
on me at last.

The *balanda* men lie stretched on the ground; they
might rest in the shade for the remainder of day. I
wonder if they realize that we have all been here
before; two seasons have passed since then — the Wet
and the Dry — so it must be more than a year ago and
I have crossed the country many times, kept moving
from one place to another by the *balanda* men always
behind me.

I wish my wife Nanggunga were here now; together
we could watch the *balanda* mob pinned down to the
ground, fighting for each tired breath. In the beginning
they were a tough lot and I would run all day long to
find, in the evening, that I was hardly a voice ahead of
them. A blackfellow alone can move through his country
like a shooting star, and not even a spear could catch
up with him, but when you are traveling with kids you
must camp and rest often, so the trackers stay close on
your heels.

From the depths of the creek valley beyond that group
of river gums comes the rattling voice of a helicopter.
From the dusty haze, left floating above the scrub after
the last willy-willy, rises a tiny dot. As the noise becomes

louder the dot quickly grows into a scavenging bird: the helicopter heads toward the gum trees, swings around them, and then with the flight of an eagle heads toward this side of the creek.

A gully packed tight with the foliage of tall trees stretches in a belt between the creek and that long ridge on the horizon. The tall grass has not yet been flattened, the scrub is still green, and the vines twining against the paperbark trunks still seem to be growing. Perhaps last year's rains went on longer than usual.

When I was here last, with Nanggunga and the children, the gully looked very dry. A blackfellow never dies of thirst in his own country, but when the trackers are at your heels there is no time to look around for water. There is a water hole, just over there, hidden in the scrub behind those huge trees. We had camped by it many times when on walkabout with *ganguman-ganguman* and it had never let us down, but last time all we found there were dry rocks. I dug deep in the ground below and found nothing but dry sand. The dark was falling fast. Down in the valley across the creek the trackers were setting up camp under the gum trees. A glimmer of light shone now and then from their fire. Nanggunga searched about for roots from which to squeeze a drop of water, but in the night . . . no, it was impossible to find any.

I crept to the white man's camp, waited hidden in the bush until late at night, and then sneaked in. A water bag was hanging from a branch as though left there to catch the cooling breeze but there was not much in it; the children drank nearly all and left hardly a handful for them to drink in the morning before we took off again. Neither lived to taste it; during the night they vomited their guts out and by morning both were dead.

Perhaps I should have speared all the *balanda* men when I was down at their camp. Even if I had got only one, the rest of the mob might have run away and not dared to follow me again — my father tried that years ago when the first prospectors came sneaking through our country; but . . . poor fellow, before he even raised his spear a dozen bullets smashed his head. From then I grew up with *ganguman-ganguman*, the grandfather, and always until the day of his death the old man begged me never to stand up against the whites. Yet, fighting or passive, both of them went to Bralgu just the same. Moony, Amsroo, Say, Sirroo, Abadja, Currong, Rarag, Eurrong — every man of our tribe has gone to Bralgu, and now I, though left till last, now I am on my way to join them.

Just above the treetops the huge hovering bird hangs in the air but instead of a rattling noise the helicopter now makes a metallic whistle and from its big belly inches a net bag with a large red cross painted across it. The load passes slowly through the crowns of the trees and comes to a stop among the top branches of the scrubby undergrowth a few feet from the ground. Inside the net bag the parcels of sweets and tobacco and the bottles of grog can be seen with the red cross stamped on them. The whites never give up, do they? Well, spirits do eat and drink all right, but not that white man's rubbish.

A plain of burned scrub and skeletons of dead casuarina trees stretch to the horizon and farther than the eye can see. It is peaceful here among these huge boulders, shady and cool. From here you can watch the willy-willy travel across country with its pole of red dust tickling the bottom of a distant cloud. The plain is still blackened from the last bush fire — it must have passed more than a year ago, but the scrub, even the wiry spinifex, has a battle to grow in this dry, sandy soil. It takes many camps to cross that plain, and only a black-fellow could make it on foot. Last time I headed this way was with Nanggunga: we had almost reached the boulders, hardly a half camp away, and the trackers were so far behind that it looked as though the whites would never make it across the plain.

Then a helicopter flew over, circled around for a while, and in a low sweep disappeared toward the horizon, leaving behind first a few puffs of smoke and a moment later peaks and hills of flame. Far beyond the machine could still be heard rattling away. The gusty wind blew burning scrub and rolls of fiery weed and grass this way and that. No time to run before the flames or even think. I crashed through the flaming wall and with Nanggunga headed toward the shelter of the boulders. My burns were bad enough . . . Poor Nanggunga, she never made it.

A film of soot still clings to the surface of the boulders — probably carried here by the wind, for there was little fire close by — rocks do not burn and this whole slope is strewn with rocks, some of them stacked taller than a tree. Now and then the white men come here in Land Rovers and chip bits of rock and dig the ground a little. Before they leave the *balanda* men often put a bundle of dynamite under one of the boulders and split it in half. Perhaps the whites think that all the goodness and worth of the blackfellow is hidden inside the rock, or maybe they blow it up in simple anger because they cannot carry it away with them.

The whites have some story about the boulders, but don't believe a word of it. The true story tells that during *midjinda* (in the beginning) a *brolga* woman traveling through the country stopped here to rest and from one of the rock shelters, Nagaiang, the Bad Spirit, rose up and crawled toward her. The woman sensed his coming and flew in the air carrying a dilly bag full of eggs. The spirit threw his spear, but missed the woman and struck only the bag; the eggs fell and as each burst open it became a heap of boulders. The dilly bag hit the ground just over there and sank deep into the earth, making a hole that is full of water all year round.

A tremor and then a blast comes from the distance and toward the horizon a cloud of dust is rising from the ground. No, it is not willy-willy, I would recognize that immediately. A faint sound of rattling machines, almost like a whisper, is carried on the wind. The *balandas* are blasting rocks to drag them away. Huge caterpillars roar about the plain, like some immense creatures risen from the depths of the sea, to crawl over the distant mountains and suddenly storm the country. It will not be long now before the whites have dug up the whole plain. It is good that I am going, for what joy could there be for me if nothing is left of my country.

When a blackfellow dies his spirit splits and goes three ways; *ganguman-ganguman* told me that one part returns to *djungunj*, the water hole right there behind the boulders, rests there, and waits to be reborn again. Another *birimbir* goes to Bralgu, land of the dead, to join our ancestors. The third spirit is the one that stays in the country to wander around and make revenge on those who have done him harm.

The blast sounds again, but much closer this time — the ground trembles like the discarded tail of a lizard. It will not be long now before they are here to level the *djungunj*. Maybe it is best that way, for rebirth into such a country would be unthinkable. Even as an insect or thistle would there be joy in growing on naked rock?

I should have left for Bralgu a long time ago; something must have gone wrong, or perhaps all that should have been done was not done. When a blackfellow dies his body has to be covered with red clay and then painted with his *djungunj* (totemic) designs, so that when he gets to Bralgu it can be seen to what tribe he belongs. In our country people gather to dance and chant — the *ubar* and the *didjeridu* play all night long and messengers are sent to every neighboring camp so all may do their part in the farewell to the dead. Our tribe numbered many but that does not help much now — someone had to be the last to go and . . . The whites — no, the *balanda* will never chant my farewell.

The helicopter is here again; it rattles in the air for

a while and then comes to rest in a space between the boulders. From the cloud of dust, and following a blackfellow tracker, come three *balandas* — the same mob that has been tracking me all the way along, but differently dressed. They move slowly as if they expect the ground to crack open beneath their feet at each step.

"Brother, drop your spear," calls one of them. Around his neck hangs a heavy cross and he keeps rubbing it gently. "We are bringing Him, Jesus, to save you." The man waits for a while, still polishing the cross, and then speaks again: "Come to us, beloved one, the Lord has a place and love for you in His Kingdom."

Another man with his face half hidden by a topee sneaks behind the boulders and whispers in a dark corner of the rock shelter: "Here, I've brought you some old clothes. There won't be anything more — the Society is mean with its welfare handout. What a pity you've paid no tax in your lifetime. Anyway do call at our shelter; cups of free tea and biscuits will be served before sunset."

He is about to say something else but the third man comes forward and pushes him aside. He is neatly dressed with a long tie, dark glasses and a curled judicial wig.

"A.I. — Amity International; stay where you are, don't come any closer. I do wish the health inspector had been here more often. These blasted flies!" He has a paper tissue held against his mouth with one hand while with the other he offers a piece of paper impaled on a pointed stick. "Sign it, quick, and . . . Don't beg for more help until you hear from the computer."

A willy-willy swings around the boulders, suddenly raising a thick column of dust, which catches the paper in its whirlpool and spirals up and away in the air. Perhaps it is . . . yes, it is *ganguman-ganguman*, or one of mighty ancestors coming from Bralgu to harry the whites. The *balanda* mob battles against the wind and beats its way to the helicopter through a mass of blown scraps, dust and weeds. The men struggle to the machine and . . . a moment later the metal bird is up in the misty air, drifting down to the depth of the plain.

A line of hills scattered with trees stretches across the horizon; one cannot see the sea from here, or even smell it. You would hardly think it is there at all except that at about dawn a bright star rises up into the sky, sent up by our ancestors from Bralgu island. Tied to a feathered string the star travels over the mainland and greets every being in the country. As the night nears its end, the star is pulled back to Bralgu until the day dawns again.

Somewhere near the middle of the line of hills is a spearhead-shaped break as if the range was an immense log chopped in two. Through that gorge during the Wet pours water from the plain heading for the sea and when a man dies his *birimbir* goes that way too. So *ganguman-ganguman* told me. On the other side of the gorge, where the river ends, a narrow piece of land squeezed between two bays stretches toward the horizon to end at last in a rocky cape. After he has traveled throughout his country the *birimbir* finally arrives there to sit on one of the boulders and wait. Then from the sea comes Nganug in his canoe, takes the spirit on board, and ferries him to Bralgu.

We seldom went to the river mouth, and I have seen that rocky cape, the hill tossed into the sea, only from a distance. When you are young there are enough places to go without sniffing along the track that in the end is to take you away from your country. *Ganguman-ganguman* used to take me fishing in other parts of the Bay, though, and we speared many *barung*, the barramundi fish, in the water and caught lobsters among the mangrove roots when the tide went down.

Whenever a blackfellow fished or gathered any tucker around the Bay, Grandfather taught me that he must make sure not to take all of it away, for when the spirits go to the Cape they might have to wait for days for Nganug to arrive and would need food during the waiting time. There can't be much tucker left around here now; so many of us have come this way and . . . Bralgu must be getting overcrowded. There are plenty of willy-willys traveling through the country nowadays; those huge clouds of dust that you see come from Bralgu too, rising from the stamping feet of our fellows making corroboree.

It won't worry me much if there aren't fish or lobsters to be found here, for behind the mangroves lie swamps full of *bralgu* (yams) — just the right tucker for a spirit, and enough of it to feed whole tribes of us; the swamps stretch as far as . . . but, they are not there any longer.

Something strange and ugly has happened here. The mangroves around the Bay have been swept away, leaving only marshy ground dotted with the remains of crumpled trees half buried in the soft ground. Here and there are piled huge heaps of soil, sand and rocks. The rocky Cape is still there, but stripped of trees and somehow shrunk; a ring of anchored ships surrounds it and only a few boulders are seen. The long strip of connecting land has been gouged away and a sharp cliff now stands in its place several spears high and still showing the raw colors of recently blasted rock. Below it the sea foams and splashes against the wall. There is no track to the Cape, not even for a *birimbir*.

The anchored ships, three of them, begin to move in a column toward the new strait; fast at first then suddenly slower, and I can see that they are loaded with freshly dug rocks. Look at the men who steer . . . yes, it's the same *balanda* mob. The man with the cross heads the column; he smiles at me and comes so close that the ship is almost touching the cliff.

"Jump on, brother, come on, I'll take you to Bralgu. There are many poor souls there, I presume, still to be converted."

Behind him sails the welfare officer and waves his topee toward the cliff: "Sorry about your family. The Queen sends her condolences; she might include you in her honors list. You know that we are about to proclaim her Queen of Bralgu too! Come on, hop aboard and show us the way to this famous island."

The Amity International man is some distance behind, moving so slowly that it would seem the ship must be about to crack under her heavy load. Steering well away from the cliff the captain leans overboard to be heard and shouts: "What thrilling news about Her Majesty. Come on aboard, and show me that island of yours. There are plenty of rocks there, I hope."

The ship suddenly hits turbulent water and as his sunglasses and wig fly off Amity International rushes back to the helm.

The ships pass through the strait, ignoring me now, and disperse toward the sunset. They might be back tomorrow or the day after if there are still some rocks left around to be hauled away. Whatever might and power they have these ships will never reach Bralgu; and tonight, as it has always happened since the first *birimbir* came to this country, the morning star will rise in the sky to bring me word from my ancestors.

Maramara

THE NIGHT has gone astray; terrible, long and ugly; it seems as though there's no end to it. Silence, that's the only thing to be heard, not just here in the tunnel but outside too — the whole world seems to have fallen into some dark sea, sunk right to the bottom of it never to rise again.

Sooner or later I will have to try and stretch upward; I might be able to get up and walk, or if not then to crawl. To lie here in this tunnel will do no good. One of my legs . . . the right one, I don't know whether it is broken or just bruised but there seems no hope of standing on it. A great heap of rocks has toppled down like a dark carcass; I feel it under my hands. It will be quite a job for me, alone, to push the rocks away and free the leg. Perhaps it might help to call, to yell or shout. Even though the whole world sounds deaf and mute, the Sergeant should be around; that one never fails to turn up, whether he's needed or not, so I'll probably hear him at any moment, jingling his keys at the tunnel gate.

Maybe the gate is open without any key to unlock it — Ngaliur has been here during the night and that gate is the only way in and out of this jail. The steel bars could not stop him; not even a concrete wall will turn him away. The whites though have never believed that Ngaliur is the one who makes all the *maramara*, all the lightning and thunder, and who tears the clouds apart to make his way down to earth and then return to the sky.

Ngaliur must have sneaked in while I was asleep, and not a sound was heard till suddenly the *maramara* blazed, and the whole tunnel, stretching for miles under the Ridge, was alight. I could see every rock and speck of dust left here by the miners so long ago. That huge fellow, that ancestor, could hardly move along the narrow tunnel — his shoulders touched the walls and his bent head scraped the ceiling. Around his knees and elbows hung rows of *galpar*, stone axes glittering with sparks as they rubbed against each other.

"See what you have done to *namanamaidj*, our country; nothing of it is left but those holes," he yelled. I wanted to say: "The whites did it, not me," but I couldn't force the words past my teeth. "You even gave our fellows to dig these rocks — a whole tribe of men."

I was dead scared; not a word, not even a thought

came to me. But even if I had said something, of what
help could that be — you don't argue with Ngaliur, even
dare to talk to him — the whites are the same to their
boss, the God.

Those rocks: maybe I could push them aside and
free the leg. It might not be broken, just bruised perhaps. It looks . . . ah! there's not only rock but dirt as
well — the mine slag heap has come down and lies on
the tunnel floor. Good I didn't say much, who could be
so cruel as to punish a poor fellow with not even enough
guts to say one word? Still, Ngaliur probably feels just
like anyone else and I think . . . yes, he must have
remembered suddenly that the whites, not me, paid with
tucker, tobacco, booze for those tunnels to be dug. When
he turned angrily, with hardly any room for him to
move — that row of axes struck against the tunnel wall
and lit the great *maramara*. He moved quickly then like
a shooting star, sprang out from the tunnel and flew
over the valley below. He would have been above the
processing plant when the lightning bolt burst and
the Mission, at the edge of the valley, the Settlement —
the whole sky blazed with light that crept into even the
tiniest corners among the rocks.

It's a pity the whites did not make the tunnel wider
when they dug for rocks, for if he'd had enough room
to move about Ngaliur would not have left such a mess
behind. He used to visit often in the evening during the
Wet, and with his *maramara* would light the whole area
with flickering white. Not much harm was done though
sometimes he hit a tree with his ax, but more often just
a branch here and there in the bush to remind us that

the boss of the country had called around again. He hit
a flagpole down at the Mission once, and split it in two,
but he never hurt a blackfellow.

This bloody leg; it feels as stiff as a log, but I must
get on. If I lean against the wall I can move it . . . No
need to hurry — inch by inch, it will take me to the
gate. Lucky I got up at all, this crooked leg is like . . .
never mind, the Sergeant, when I find him, will help
me. All that magic stuff he carries in the little box with
the red cross that cures the lot. He even helped me, once,
to recover from a snakebite.

Yes, he will pull me out of this, I've done good turns
for him. No white man knows how to track and without
me the Sergeant would not have been able to catch
even a buffalo. Whenever a blackfellow got out of hand
we had to follow him; chase the poor bugger for days
sometimes but the Sergeant would never come back
without his prisoner. That's how they kept all our fellows
here to carve those tunnels and haul the rocks from
the belly of the Ridge.

Down in the valley below the Ridge a crusher used
to work night and day, rumbling like an immense beast
swallowing its prey and then puffing a cloud of grayish
dust which spread over the whole *namanamaidj*, the
tribal country.

There's some light at last — that must be the tunnel's end. It's still a long way to drag this stiff leg, but
I'll make it. I can't see the gate or the steel bars so
perhaps it's the light of a torch — the Sergeant coming
with his torch to look for me. He comes to the gate every
morning to let me out and in the evening I come back

again; this is the best spot to stay for the night where you can be dead drunk, full of petrol fumes you've sniffed or just mad in your own way, but without any whites to kick you around. "Sneak in and save trouble for both of us," the Sergeant always said, and as soon as he let me through the gate I would begin to feel the warmth of the earth; it is like crawling under a blanket — the deeper you go, the darker and warmer it becomes. It could be a six-dog night outside* but under the Ridge nothing troubles you.

The Sergeant isn't here; the light is not his torch but the flames of a campfire and the Gunwingu men, Starra, Lurr, Aroona, Uralla, Galang, Honka, Thoar, Eyerah, Rob — the whole tribe is gathered around.

"Come and join us, we are your mob," calls Starra, the oldest among them.

"Have they chucked you out too?" asks Lurr. "What is the use of hanging around any longer — the whites don't give us booze anymore."

Aroona, his body painted with clay, comes forward. "Ngaliur got the whites at last; the crusher, the processing plant, the whole settlement — flattened."

"He made just one lightning sweep, nothing more," says Uralla, the youngest among them, dancing as he speaks.

Next to him is Galang with the cockatoo feather headdress. "Come and dance with us, it is the big *bugamani* time. We have to mourn our fellows — a

---

* Aborigines measure the cold by the number of dogs needed to keep you warm.

whole tribe. Let us dance and sing for them. The whites are gone forever and it is our *namanamaidj* again."

Thoar, busy beating a palm frond against a *ubar* log, pauses for a moment: "There's not a single white fellow left for a dozen camps around."

Eyerah comes close and leans so near that every single line of the tribal signs scored on the skin of his chest is clearly seen: "You haven't forgotten our *bugamani*, come and dance — the whites will never be back."

Rob stops blowing the *didjeridu* to catch his breath: "Ngaliur finished the whole lot; only the mushroom-shaped cloud he left is still there, lying thick over the Settlement."

With a shout all the fellows begin to dance, stamping their feet till a cloud of dust rises up and is sucked with the swaying men into the tunnel toward the inmost depths of the Ridge. Now and then a voice rises above the chant calling me to follow; if it weren't for this bloody leg I could run and catch them up but no, they won't wait. The light is fading and even the faint sounds of the *didjeridu* and *ubar* I could hear have died away now.

I should have followed them. After all I've done I still belong with those people. They'd never say anything to harm me, you never curse a fellow from your own mob — even though the whole tribe resented my meddling in the whites' business. The women disliked me and often, to silence their children, they threatened to call me to give the naughty child to the whites.

There are no more large rocks on the ground here, the

tunnel floor is only dust. I must have come farther than Ngaliur for it seems he did not shake this part of the Ridge. I'd better turn back toward the gate; it could be open — Ngaliur might have knocked it on his way in and out. I wish . . . no I can't curse him, or those fellows who left me behind. My own decisions have led me this way. I always thought Helen, the nurse, would take me with her when she left the Mission — it was she who taught me how to hold a knife and fork. Every Sunday it was, after Mass, but it took her almost a year to get rid of my habit of sucking up tea so loudly. Whenever she wanted to tour around the country I was the only one trusted to show her our *namanamaidj*. Always she carried a large dilly bag and on our return she had filled it with small rocks — I wondered why she wanted them; maybe for magic as women often do, or to make white men's medicine, but I was too shy to ask. ᵖᵍ· 77

Just a moment . . . the tunnel . . . no, it's not the end, only a branch. I can feel the corners with my fingers but I wonder which way to take now. No one has ever told me about this junction — I doubt if the Sergeant knows about it. But perhaps he does for he warned me not to wander around and get lost almost every time he let me into the tunnel for the night. I only went far enough to shelter from the draft of the gateway and be warm; some nights were so bitter you would need a whole mob of dogs to keep you from shivering. In the morning, when he let me out, the Sergeant often asked: "You didn't try to find another way out? Most of your mob disappeared that way."

The Ridge above the tunnel stretches all the way

along the Jingana River, and most of it hollow by now since the whites have dragged out so much rock — uranium, they call it — taken it all down to the valley to feed the crusher and the machines at the processing plant. The whites would still be around here digging under the Ridge if they hadn't found a better place — high up on the mountain. It's a whole plain littered with gray rocks to be gathered right from the ground without the bother of burrowing tunnels through the hill. Before they left here, though, the whites put a barred gate across the tunnel mouth and gave the key to the Sergeant. So he's the boss of the lot now.

So many of our people went in — but I never saw one come out — maybe there *is* another way to leave the tunnel; perhaps after wandering around in the darkness you spring out into the sunshine on the other side of the Ridge. If a fellow should walk out there he'd head straight for the bush and never be seen around here again.

The way has grown steep here; I'd better move slowly or I'll hurt that poor leg again. The tunnel is so narrow, now, that my shoulders are touching both walls. I am holding on to the rough edges of rocks, as I move slowly, so as not to slip. The walls feel . . . wet, or perhaps just cold, I am not sure which.

This might be a passage right down to the *maraiin* cave; that's good if it is, for from there I have only to follow the course of the Jingana River and it will lead me to the Settlement. It's quite a long way to walk, but it's Gunwingu country all the way, so I couldn't go astray.

The elders say that during the Dreamtime the Rainbow Serpent Jingana came down from a rain cloud and crawled through our *namanamaidj*, leaving a deep gorge in her track. The journey lasted three days and wherever she camped she pissed, leaving behind large pools of water, which are still there, and never go dry all year round. At the end of the journey Jingana crawled into the ground under the high plain, hollowing out a deep cave at the top end of the gorge.

Only grown men went along the Jingana Gorge to hold ceremonies and returned telling nothing. The youngsters and women stayed away from there but Helen couldn't understand that, laughed aloud when I warned her. It didn't worry her. Jingana was not her *maraiin*, and meant her no harm. She even went swimming in one of the pools and tried to drag me into the water too — not that I wouldn't have liked to join her, naked as she was, but the whole gorge, the trees, the rocks . . . everything there is *maraiin*. Even the fish, the turtles and the crocodiles must not be touched.

The tunnel has narrowed into a burrow and I have to squeeze between the rocks, crawling on my elbows. The leg doesn't hurt much now; I could almost forget about it except for the sharp edges of the rock that hide in the darkness and claw at the wound.

It can't be much farther now; how many fellows must have gone this way — women and children too — that the Sergeant had locked in. You only had to take a loaf of bread, or walk through the bush around the mining site (the whites call it trespassing), or search through the rubbish behind the Settlement and you would end up here in the tunnel. It's a pity I didn't join them long ago; I would have been easier in my mind among my own kind. Even if there is nothing great to hope for there is warmth and comfort among your own folk.

This tunnel seems endless. I should come to the cave very soon. When I went there with Helen it didn't seem so far, but of course we went the other way, along the gorge to the top of the river. I tried to explain to Helen that no man should ever go into the cave and annoy the Jingana Serpent, but she listened to none of it. I should have known, for no matter what you feel or say, the whites will always go their own way. Helen carried a hammer and kept chipping bits of rock here and there as we walked. We wandered through the cave for hours, with a torch showing our way, and though I begged her not to make so much noise with her hammer, Helen scarcely heard my words.

The tunnel is much wider now; I can walk freely and there are few rocks underfoot. A glimmer of light comes from somewhere and . . . A group of people is gathered around a dying campfire; they lie stretched on the tunnel floor, where I will step on them unless I tread carefully.

An old woman rises up supported by *djad*, a digging stick, and stretches her hand out to me. She is offering a piece of sweet potato, still coated in ash from the fire: "Have it. It's still warm. It's not much but there's no more — I had to split one *gugu* for the whole tribe."

From the darkness steps a boy shielding his face with

one hand and holding a box of chocolates in the other: "Give this back to Sergeant," he whispers. "Then perhaps he'll set me free."

With his back against the wall sits a man, his head partly hidden under a miner's hat and his hands around the neck of a wine flagon: "Have a drink," he calls and raises the flagon toward me. "I am your *wala*, your elder brother, you know. Drink with me."

Two young women come staggering along the tunnel to stop hardly a foot in front of me, trembling and swaying. My *ngalinga*, my two nieces, are these. One has sores upon her face and has lost most of her hair; the other bears the scars of a broken bottle on her bosom. They stand here in front of me, trying to speak but saying nothing until — "Big brawl at miners' camp . . . again . . ." one mumbles at last.

Farther up the tunnel a queue of boys sidles up to a large petrol drum. Each awaits his turn to press his mouth against the opening of the drum and sniff, for just a moment, the desirable, dizzying fumes. His poor brain will be numbed for hours afterward; he may even sink into an unnatural sleep.

This woman who sits and sobs is my *djala*, my sister. In front of her, stretched out on a plastic bag, lies the naked body of a child, shrouded in a swarm of buzzing flies. "Your friend the nurse gave him a biscuit and he died soon after."

From a pool of darkness comes a pair of hands. They skim through the shadows like a shooting star over the dark sky and stop in front of my face bringing a dilly bag full of rocks: "Give it to your friend, the nurse," says a voice from the dark.

I didn't see much more of Helen, not for years, for soon after that trip to Jingana Cave she packed her bags, stuffed them with bits of rock, and left in a hurry. I thought she would never come back; the whites are like that — they come here, sniff around, peep into our life, and then go away never to be seen or heard of again. Helen did come back though, once, just after the surveyors had been all over the country and put up signboards reading LEASED LAND TRESPASSERS WILL BE PROSECUTED wherever they went. It was cruel, not so much for me but for the elders, who could go no more into the Jingana Gorge to hold their ceremonies. Whenever they tried to sneak up there the Sergeant and his white mob would round them up, and since the tunnel was not yet dug to provide a lockup for blackfellows, he would chain them for days under the big banyan tree in his camp.

The tunnel has narrowed again; I can hardly squeeze between the rocks . . . But far away, at the end of this long burrow, a handful of faint light shows itself to me.

Helen came back to open a new church down at the Mission. Quite a building, all of steel and glass with an immense cross stretching right into the cloud; perhaps that was so the angels when they came to kiss it would not be stared at. Very few people called Helen by her name — the people from the mining settlement always called her "Boss," and to honor the "Boss" we had to decorate all the trees at the Mission with paper crosses and flags, and each of us was given a cloth to wear around his waist.

The elders begged me to ask Helen that all the survey pegs and signs be removed from Jingana Gorge. Maybe she could have done something, but I never got the chance to talk to her. Just before she arrived the Sergeant flew me and a few others in the helicopter, far beyond our *namanamaidj*, and left us in the bush. It didn't seem so far, only an hour or two in the machine, but it took us days to walk back. Even if I had talked to Helen, and she had been willing to help us, those white miners are so mad on uranium rock, I'm pretty sure they wouldn't have been persuaded to give it up.

A tiny blade of light squeezes through a crack in the stone and slices the dark mass in two. An opening . . . no, it's too small for me to crawl through, but . . . Look, I can get my head out, see the day outside at last. It is misty — chilly and silent. Down in the valley still sits the mushroom cloud; the immense white stepping-stone by which Ngaliur climbed back into the sky. He's done a good job down there — the whole valley is swept clean like the palm of my hand. Even the heaps of uranium ore around the crusher have been blown away. Right down at the foot of the Ridge some part of a building has been torn apart and driven into the ground and entangled in it is . . . yes, it's the cross from the church roof twisted into a crazy shape and flattened against the rocks.

The whites must have really angered Ngaliur. He's struck many times before but never with such rage and he won't need to call again for a long time to come.

Mogo, the Crocodile Man

THE RIVER HAS RISEN — it has swollen up overnight like a deep wound, rolled over its banks and spread through Kakadu country. It has swallowed not only the land but even the remaining patches of spear grass and scrub. Only the trunks of dead trees are to be seen here and there rising above the flooding murk and stretching toward the misty sky.

No end to the water; I wonder if Mogo knows it. He lies coiled up on the floor of the boat with his arms pressed firmly against his belly. It must hurt; he has hardly moved since I helped him get in. Galba, the dog, stares all the time and squeaks now and then. The animal has been with us since he was a pup, but never has he behaved so strangely. Suddenly the dog senses something, props up against me and claws my shoulder. Perhaps I should move quicker — the paddles are hard and heavy, I am clumsy. Whatever I do the blades either flash through the air or dive into the water. Even if I push hard with all my weight, the boat hardly moves.

Easy, I should move gently; to rock the boat will do no good. Poor Mogo, he has had a tough time, last night his belly was so upset, he nearly threw up all his guts. He thinks *ganguri*, the yam I cooked him on hot ash, buggered his belly.

"You got it from the swamp near the river, a bloody pond full of murk," he yelled, nursing his belly. He will get over it, I thought at first. Mogo has been in the bush too long, for even though white, his skin has grown tough and thick like an iguana's — there is nothing around that will hurt him. "That stinking yam, it has bloody knocked me. Get that boat, take me out of this hell."

A branch of dead tree floats on the dark, muddy water and drifts slowly down the stream. The water pushes the boat too and sweeps it off its course; it should be moving straight across to the other bank but if the boat ever reaches the other end of water it will be somewhere far down the river. Why worry — Mogo did not tell me where to paddle him. I reckon he wanted to go back to his white mob, but it is the Wet — the whites do not stay around here to be bogged; they have gone back to their own country. Maybe . . . yes, there is a homestead somewhere there across the river, but it must be many camps away and the boat will never get so far.

It could not be because of *ganguri*, the yam; something else must have gone wrong. Perhaps *mangorang*, a spell, has been put on Mogo. I saw no one hanging around our camp, but the spirits are always about — you live as long as one of them wishes before he decides to send you off. If it were not for that the people would live longer than trees or rocks; no man would ever go back to Dreaming.

Mogo should know all about *mangorang*; he has been here for ages. I was only *djungun*, a girl, when he first came to Kakadu country and I know I could have been *maga*, a grandmother, long ago if my children and the tribe had lived long enough. He came looking for crocodiles. He had two boats and with his younger brother he roamed the river. They went far down to the mangroves near the sea and all the way upstream to the foot of the hills; they even moved into Wuningag country now and then. All my brothers — Goongwar, Erad, Nagi, Orong and Coonmidjendar — and my sons — Ijawu, Dala and Eake — worked for him. The boys helped to make the camp, set the nets, they even shot the crocodiles, dragged the beasts from the water and skinned them. They hung on to Mogo's brother often; I could not tell then why they liked the younger fellow. The boys called him Woragid, a white rock, and . . . yes, after the crocodile skins had dried in the sun and were piled up on the truck, he would pick up two of the boys, whistle to them to jump on top of the load, and drive off to the hills. There is no way of crossing the river by car down here in the low country, not even during the Dry. They took the skins by serpent track winding high up into the hills and then stretching over Wuningag country — it took days to go and come back.

A handful of water is splashed into the boat and sprinkles Mogo's skin. He hardly notices it, only shivers slightly; but Galba, the dog, quickly jumps up, looks for a moment on the drops of water on Mogo's arm, and with a few licks of his tongue mops them up.

Mogo does not look strange any longer. His skin, which used to be white like an ant's when he came first, darkened after a few seasons. He thinks it is all because of the sun, but I reckon it came from living with us for so long — he is already halfway to becoming a black-fellow. Yes, that could be what annoyed his Spirit Boss, God or Good he calls him. That Spirit did not like Mogo becoming one of us and made *mangorang* to get him back to the white man's world.

I wonder will Woragid, his brother, go the same way. He too mixed with blackfellows a lot. Whenever he came back from town he brought a half truckload of grog; our boys used to follow him around like a swarm of flies and got a bottle now and then. Mogo did not say much, he also had a bottle now and then. He only got cranky about *griga*, a small box his brother brought back from town. Woragid carried it hanging down from his shoulders and it used to make a cheeping sound; it looked as though there was a pigeon from stone country locked in it.

The boys told me the *griga* box helped Woragid to find the right rocks that he was after in the bush. I wondered how it could track anything; the box had no eyes and no nose to sniff with. Yet he got it to cheep somehow and it led him all over the country until at last it took him high up into the hills.

A stone forest of bark-stripped trees plunges down almost to where the branches rest still and silent on the flood. The boat must have drifted quite a way down the river, swung around the score of trunks, and come to a stop with its bow caught up in the fork of a tree. I should rest for a while, no need to press hard, God or Good could wait. I must be near the swamp now, half-way between our camp and the sea. Nowhere in the whole country do the paperbark trees grow taller. You could put both arms around the trunk and yet not encircle it. In the shade under the trees the ground used to be wet throughout the Dry. You could find yams here all year round; they grew as big as buffalo horns. The crocodiles sneaked in from the nearby river and hid around the pools under a green canopy of leaves. Mogo never shot here; he thought the crocodiles sneaked into the paperbark swamp to lay their eggs and he left them in peace so that their young could hatch.

Things have changed a lot lately though. After Mogo's brother Woragid took to the hills with that *griga* box nothing came well any longer. He made a big camp high up in Wuningag country; lots of white fellows got in and the mob did something very nasty to the river. The crabs would not stay in the water, they crawled out on the banks and lay half sunk in mud with their eyes stuck wide open. Swarms of fish turned over on their bellies and let themselves float down the river to the sea.

A huge paperbark tree came down with a sudden crash and the branches left a wide gap. The trunk smashed into the water and made the waves splash against the boat. The bow moved away from the fork of the tree and the boat slid back again into the current. The crushing noise must have upset the dog; the animal suddenly grows restless and begins to claw me; it shivers and its hair stands on end, perhaps it is afraid not only for Mogo or me but of being taken across the water. Not far away, a buffalo carcass floats down the stream; it is quite large and sways now and then. I have seen none for years. Before, whole herds used to roam the bush and during the Dry come down to the swamp and hang around the green area. The stockmen from faraway homesteads often used to call, fly over the bush in a helicopter, chase the buffalo across the river and trap them. Anyhow, they stopped calling in long ago.

There is more of a current now; it pushes the boat faster and turns it this way and that. Up in Wuningag country there has been a lot of rain. I wonder what Woragid with that *griga* box and his white mob did to the river; after each flood the whole strip of land from the hills right down to the sea is strange. The trees and grass die soon after and instead of new growth coming up, the ground remains covered with dark murk.

Mogo should have done something. I begged him often to go up into the hills and ask his brother not to murk the river anymore. Perhaps Woragid did it because his elder brother was nasty about the *griga* box and laughed about it. However, Mogo grew angry whenever I said anything and did not talk to me for days afterward. I asked the boys to see to it. Goongwar, Erad, Nagi,

Orong, Coonmidjendar, Ijawu, Dala and Eake all went there, but what could blackfellows do about it — the Wuningag country had changed into an anthill full of whites leveling the hills and dragging out the rocks. At break of day, the boys said, a cloud of dust rises, darkens the sun until evening, and then slowly settles down on the ground until the first rain washes it out. It was not right to ask them to go, for even if all our mighty ancestors suddenly rose all together they could never muster enough spears to chase the whites away.

A pandanus tree tangled with barbed wire, old truck tires, waste drums and branches came fast down the river. It was headed straight toward me when suddenly it stopped for the moment, perhaps it had hit a hidden snag, then floated on downstream. It passed close to the bow. Caught up in the wire and branches a man's head is seen; it pops out of the water now and then. It could be Goongwar, Erad, Nagi, Orong, Coonmidjendar, Ijawu, Dala or Eake, any of them. The boys went up to hang around the white men's camp and have not been back for years now.

I should tell Mogo about the man carried down the river, to whom else can I talk? Let him rest and wait until he wakes up. His belly must have given him a hard time; his face is pale like ash and stiff — perhaps he still suffers pain even though asleep. The dog stares at him no more. The animal crouches on the side of the boat and looks into the distance, it howls, then is quiet until the sound fades away far down the river behind the edge of the dead mangrove forest, then he repeats the call.

The flood stretches away endlessly — there is no sight of land, only here and there the upper branch of a tree thrusts up above the water. Perhaps the flood has extended even farther than the homestead and gone right through the white man's land. There might be no more land left, only this water, so muddy that not even leeches will live in it. It seems to be endless. Whatever has happened to the land, that Good or God should be here to take Mogo? Maybe he is sitting on the branch of one of these trees, with a rope in his hand. As soon as we come close he will throw it down, make a noose around Mogo's body and pull him up — the way the boys pulled a crocodile out of the water when they had shot it.

We will part only for a while. Mogo is used to staying with us, he hates white man's tucker and likes to live in the bush by a campfire. He will be back. When he comes to life again, he could be a bird . . . no, he will turn up as a crocodile, swim quickly out of this murk and swim over the sea to one of the islands — no harm will ever come to him there.

Galba, the dog, does not howl any longer; he has come closer to me and leans his head against my arm. We have to beat our way back across the river and find some Kakadu country left somewhere — not big, but enough to make a campfire, cook *ganguri* on hot ash, and rest.

Glossary

badbad — boulders
bad-maraiin — totem rock
balanda men — white men
barang — barramundi fish
birimbir — spirit
bongaru — human-hair belt
Bralgu — mythological island, land of the dead
bralgu — yams
brolga — bird of gracious behavior about the size of a
        turkey, known as *Grus rubicunda*
bugamani — mourning ceremony
buidjub — digging stick
cunda stick — fighting stick
didjeridu — immense, deep-noted wind instrument
        made from up to eight feet of hollow tree
diridi — hawk
djad — yam (digging) stick

GLOSSARY

djala — sister
djamar — feather headdress
djinabano — buffalo
djungun — unmarried girl
djungunj — sacred water hole inherited matrilineally; totemic designs
dodoro — pigeon
Dreamtime or Dreaming — myth of creation
dua country — paternal tribal country
duladna — soft bark
galpar — stone axes
ganguman-ganguman — grandfather
ganguri — yam
griga — Geiger counter
gugu — sweet potato
gungi — rainmaking dance
jiritja country — maternal tribal country
kunapipi — fertility ceremony
maga — grandmother
mangal — spear thrower
mangorang — spell
maraiin — manhood ceremony (sacred)
marain poles — surveyor's pegs
maramara — lightning and thunder
margidju — native doctor
midjinda — beginning
miringu — revenge
murga — dilly bag
namanamaidj — native country
nauaran — snake
ngalinga — nieces
ubar — musical instrument
wala — elder brother
womara — tortoise shell